A Whale of a Tail

A Whales and Tails Mystery

by

Kathi Daley

Books by Kathi Daley
Come for the murder, stay for the romance.

Zoe Donovan Cozy Mystery:
Halloween Hijinks
The Trouble With Turkeys
Christmas Crazy
Cupid's Curse
Big Bunny Bump-off
Beach Blanket Barbie
Maui Madness
Derby Divas
Haunted Hamlet
Turkeys, Tuxes, and Tabbies
Christmas Cozy
Alaskan Alliance
Matrimony Meltdown
Soul Surrender
Heavenly Honeymoon
Hopscotch Homicide
Ghostly Graveyard
Santa Sleuth
Shamrock Shenanigans
Kitten Kaboodle
Costume Catastrophe
Candy Cane Caper
Holiday Hangover
Easter Escapade
Camp Carter
Trick or Treason
Reindeer Roundup
Hippity Hoppity Homicide

Firework Fiasco
Henderson House
Holiday Hostage
Lunacy Lake
Celtic Christmas – *December 2019*

Zimmerman Academy The New Normal
Zimmerman Academy New Beginnings
Ashton Falls Cozy Cookbook

Tj Jensen Paradise Lake Mystery:
Pumpkins in Paradise
Snowmen in Paradise
Bikinis in Paradise
Christmas in Paradise
Puppies in Paradise
Halloween in Paradise
Treasure in Paradise
Fireworks in Paradise
Beaches in Paradise
Thanksgiving in Paradise – *Fall 2019*

Whales and Tails Cozy Mystery:
Romeow and Juliet
The Mad Catter
Grimm's Furry Tail
Much Ado About Felines
Legend of Tabby Hollow
Cat of Christmas Past
A Tale of Two Tabbies
The Great Catsby
Count Catula
The Cat of Christmas Present

A Winter's Tail
The Taming of the Tabby
Frankencat
The Cat of Christmas Future
Farewell to Felines
A Whisker in Time
The Catsgiving Feast
A Whale of a Tail
The Catnap Before Christmas – *December 2019*

Writers' Retreat Mystery:
First Case
Second Look
Third Strike
Fourth Victim
Fifth Night
Sixth Cabin
Seventh Chapter
Eighth Witness
Ninth Grave

Rescue Alaska Mystery:
Finding Justice
Finding Answers
Finding Courage
Finding Christmas
Finding Shelter – *Fall 2019*

A Tess and Tilly Mystery:
The Christmas Letter
The Valentine Mystery
The Mother's Day Mishap
The Halloween House

The Thanksgiving Trip
The Saint Paddy's Promise
The Halloween Haunting – *Fall 2019*

The Inn at Holiday Bay:

Boxes in the Basement
Letters in the Library
Message in the Mantel
Answers in the Attic
Haunting in the Hallway – *August 2019*
Pilgrim in the Parlor – *October 2019*
Note in the Nutcracker – *December 2019*

The Hathaway Sisters:

Harper
Harlow

Haunting by the Sea:

Homecoming by the Sea
Secrets by the Sea
Missing by the Sea
Betrayal by the Sea
Christmas by the Sea – *Fall 2019*

Sand and Sea Hawaiian Mystery:

Murder at Dolphin Bay
Murder at Sunrise Beach
Murder at the Witching Hour
Murder at Christmas

Murder at Turtle Cove
Murder at Water's Edge
Murder at Midnight
Murder at Pope Investigations – *July 2019*

Seacliff High Mystery:
The Secret
The Curse
The Relic
The Conspiracy
The Grudge
The Shadow
The Haunting

Road to Christmas Romance:
Road to Christmas Past

Chapter 1

Tuesday, October 22

The best stories, I've learned with time, seem to exist within the crossroads of fact and fiction.

"Welcome, everyone," I greeted the group of men and women who had shown up for the Tuesday night Mystery Lovers Book Club. "I'm thrilled to see so many new faces in the crowd. My name is Caitlin Hart West." It still felt odd using my new married surname. I glanced to my left. "This is my best friend and business partner, Tara O'Brian. We would both like to welcome our guest speaker, Winifred Westminster, to Coffee Cat Books. Winnifred pens novels in a variety of genres, including true crime, thriller, and traditional mystery." I paused as the group applauded. "Winifred, who prefers to be referred to as Winnie, will be releasing a novel this Christmas. The novel is based on the real-life murder of Amy Anderson, a Madrona Island native who died almost fifteen years ago." I paused to let that sink in. Tara and I had both gone to the same high school as Amy, although she'd been two years older, and we'd both been at the party following the homecoming game at which Amy died. To say that Amy Anderson's murder hit close to home was putting it mildly, and while I had mixed feelings about Winnie exploiting the tragedy, I knew our patrons would be interested in hearing what she had to say, so when she asked to make a stop at Coffee Cat Books during her prepublication publicity tour, Tara and I had decided to welcome her. "I am going to turn the floor over to Winnie," I continued, "but first, I'd like to remind everyone to hold their comments and questions until the end."

I stepped aside, and Winifred took the stage, which was really just a slightly raised platform my husband, Cody West, had built for the occasion. We'd transformed the lounge of Coffee Cat Books, the bookstore/coffee bar/cat lounge Tara and I owned, into an auditorium of sorts for our very special speaker, who had gained the interest of readers from as far away as Seattle.

"Thank you for having me," Winnie said after taking the floor. "The story of Amy Anderson is one I have been working on for a very long time. Amy was a high school student here on the island when she was brutally murdered while attending a party following the homecoming game fifteen years ago. The death of this delightful girl hit the community hard, but I think it hit me harder than most because I'd first met Amy during a very difficult time in my own history and her sunny disposition had helped me to move on and take a second chance on life."

Winnie paused before she continued. She seemed to be a good storyteller who understood the art of pacing. Eventually, she continued in a slightly lower tone of voice. "My story opens where many good mysteries begin, on a dark and stormy night, this one in October almost thirty years ago. I first came to this island after my dear husband, Vinnie, passed away unexpectedly. Twenty-two was much too young to be a widow, and I found myself not only heartbroken but also completely lost and alone. I can still remember sitting in a dark house on my first night on the island. A storm had rolled in, and I watched in silence as the sky flashed with lightning and rain poured down over the angry sea."

Winnie took a sip of water and slowly looked around the room. It seemed she had much of the audience on the edge of their seats. "The house I'd rented for the summer was a large old thing. Not only were there two stories of living space, but there was a finished attic, which some past resident had used for storage, and a dank and damp, unfinished basement. The wind pounded the structure as it blew in from the sea, and the walls swayed under the force of it all. It entered my mind that the storm might very well bring the whole house down around me, but at the time, I didn't care. Death, I'd already decided, would be a welcome reprieve from the life I now envisioned for myself."

I couldn't imagine how difficult it must be to lose the person you most depended on. The person who was to play a starring role in your future. The person who gave that future meaning. I tried to imagine life without Cody, but all I could imagine was darkness and despair. I supposed I could understand how, in that moment, Winnie really hadn't cared if she lived or died. I supposed that in a similar situation, I might not either. But Winnie had survived and thrived, and I guess I knew that if forced to face a life of darkness, I would find my way back to the light as well.

Winnie continued. "I remember grieving for everything I had lost as the storm battered the island. I remember wondering if I had the strength to endure another day. I remember holding the bottle of sedatives I'd been prescribed and considering the options when I heard a noise that sounded a lot like someone crying. I was sure I was alone in the house, but it sounded so real. I listened for a moment but couldn't tell what I was hearing, so I decided to take a look around. I began by exploring the main floor of living space, but when I didn't find anything that would explain the crying, I headed down the stairs to the basement, where I found a little girl who couldn't be more than four or five sitting in the middle of the unfinished room sobbing. I asked her who she was and how she had gotten there, and she shared that her name was Amy and that she had followed her cat into the basement through an air vent that led to the outside. I asked her why she was crying, and she said that her cat had disappeared and she couldn't find the crawlspace leading to the small opening that would allow her to get out of the room. I'd just moved in and wasn't aware of an exterior access point, so I picked up the child, took her upstairs, and then carried her to the house next door, where her mother was baking. The poor woman was a mess when she found out that Amy wasn't upstairs taking a nap as she'd thought. She offered me a cup of tea. We got to talking and suddenly the dark and empty space that had been my life since Vinnie died, seemed a little brighter. From that moment, I knew I'd found a surrogate family of sorts. At least for the summer. Amy was such a cute little thing. She would come over to my house to visit with me, sometimes bringing flowers she'd picked from her mother's garden. I wasn't normally much of a baker, but that summer. I always made sure I had plenty of homemade cookies for Amy when she came by."

"So what happened?" one of the women in the audience asked. "After that summer?"

"I returned to my old life. When I'd arrived on Madrona Island, I'd been a broken woman, but after the long summer here, and the companionship of this very special little girl, I felt ready to rebuild the life I'd left behind. I came back to the island the following summer and a few times after that, but then I published my first book and began to spend time developing my career. My visits became shorter and less frequent, and eventually, my life as a writer took over, and I stopped coming altogether. I usually remembered to send Amy a card for her birthday, and I made a point of sending a package around the holidays, but I will admit we lost touch as the years went by. I'm sure my relationship with the child I'd found on that rainy day would have faded into a distant memory if left to decay naturally over time, but then I learned of Amy's brutal death, and what had been a warm and pleasant memory turned into something dark and filled with rage."

"Who killed her? And why?" another of the women asked.

"I didn't know for a very long time. No one did. But then I came to the island a year and a half ago to spend some time with my thoughts after my life became hectic once again. I happened to run into a woman I'd met when I'd visited the island all those years ago, and we got to talking. She mentioned something about Amy and the events leading up to her death, which got me to thinking. I latched onto an idea that had popped into my head and began to dig around a bit. Eventually, I stumbled on to something that led me to the answer I'd been seeking. Once I began to puzzle things through, I realized I'd happened across a clue, which then led to another clue, which finally led to the answer.

"So who did it? Who killed Amy?" the woman asked once again.

"If you want the answer to that question, you will need to read the book."

I had a feeling that Winnie was going to sell a lot of books. Not only had the presentation she'd provided for our customers been completely captivating but if she had solved the murder, I knew that everyone, including the resident deputy, my brother-in-law, Ryan Finnegan, was going to be interested in learning the answer no one had been able to find to this point.

"So you figured out who killed Amy and haven't told anyone?" The same woman appeared to be beyond shocked.

Winnie bobbed her head. "As I've already said, the answer to the question of who murdered Amy Anderson will be revealed when the book is published."

"But you are giving the killer time to get away," the woman insisted.

I found I had to agree with that, but while Winnie was willing to answer questions after her presentation, she refused to give away the ending of her book no matter how many people asked. In a way, I could see why she would want to keep that to herself until the book was published, but it seemed wrong to me that she had figured out the answer to a fifteen-year-old old murder yet hadn't shared that information with anyone, including Amy's parents and law enforcement.

After everyone left, Tara and I began cleaning up.

"So, what did you make of the presentation?" she asked as the first of many raindrops began to hit the wall of windows that overlooked the dark sea.

"Winnie certainly is a good storyteller, and she seemed to be able to draw every single person in the room into her tale, but I do wonder how she solved a murder no one has been able to figure out in the past fifteen years."

Tara folded one of the chairs and added it to the stack to return to the storage room. "Yeah. I did find myself wondering about the specifics of the whole thing. I mean, if she has identified the killer, shouldn't she have at the very least told Finn what she knows? And even if she didn't want Finn to ruin her big reveal, doesn't it seem dangerous to taunt the killer with the fact that he or she has been identified and it is only a matter of time before their secret is known?"

"It does seem as if she is traveling a dangerous road," I agreed.

"When Winnie asked to speak to our club, I knew she had been working on a novel based on the story of Amy's death, but I had no idea she'd actually solved the murder. I wonder if Finn knows."

"I guess we can ask him. Siobhan mentioned that they had a babysitter and she and Finn were going to O'Malley's for dinner and drinks," I referred to my older sister. "They might still be there."

O'Malley's was the bar my two brothers, Aiden and Danny, had bought and refurbished.

"I wouldn't mind a drink," Tara said.

"Cody is in Florida with his mother until tomorrow, so I have no reason to hurry home. If Winnie really has figured out what happened to Amy and isn't just making this whole thing up to sell more books, I would think Finn would insist that she share that information with him."

"I'm not sure he can force her to tell him anything she has dug up, but there is the whole withholding evidence thing they always talk about on the cop shows I enjoy on TV, so maybe. Let's finish up here and then head to O'Malley's. I wanted to talk to Danny anyway. He wants to throw a Halloween party at the bar and asked me if I would help him with the food and decorations."

"It's nice of you to help."

Tara shrugged. "I don't mind, and he is letting us use the bar for the party following the homecoming game on Saturday. It seems that a lot of alumni plan to be in town this year. It will be good to catch up with everyone."

"I was talking to Owen Nelson about doing a photo of my cabin for the wall over the fireplace in the new house, and he mentioned that Archie planned to be in town this year." Owen Nelson had been introverted and socially awkward in high school and had never really fit in with the popular crowd. He hadn't been supersmart like his friends, but he had been a talented photographer who'd worked on both the yearbook and the school newspaper. After he graduated, he went on to open his own photography studio and seemed to be doing very well. His best friends in high school had been Archie Baldwin, a computer geek who went on to work for the NSA, and Becky Bollinger, another computer geek, who went on to own a major software company. Both Archie and Becky had moved off the island after graduation.

"Is Becky coming as well?" Tara asked. In high school, Owen, Archie, and Becky had been inseparable. Most referred to them as the Three Nerdsketeers.

"He wasn't sure. He hoped Becky could make it, but her software company has grown a lot over the past two years, so she is pretty busy."

"I heard she is doing really well. I hope she can make it. It would be fun to catch up. We need to be sure to get the word out about the party at the bar. Owen, Archie, and Becky were in Danny and Cody's class, but I'm going to be sure to invite those alumni who are still around from our class as well." Tara began turning off the lights. "I've heard they are expecting to have a good turnout for the game this year."

"I've noticed that homecoming games played in October have a better turnout than the ones in September. I've also noticed that alumni are more apt to come back for the first few games after graduation, but then their attendance tapers off." I checked to make sure the coffee machines were cleaned and ready for the morning. "It will be good to see whoever shows."

As soon as Tara and I finished cleaning up, we headed to the bar. Weekdays in the off-season tended to be slow, so other than a few regulars sitting at the bar, the place was mostly empty. Finn and Siobhan were sitting at the far end of the long, horseshoe-shaped bar, chatting with Danny and Aiden, and Tara and I joined them.

"How was the author presentation?" Siobhan asked as I slid onto a stool next to her.

"Interesting." I leaned in a bit so I could see Finn, who was sitting on her other side. "Winnie Westminster told the group that she had solved the Amy Anderson murder and would reveal the killer in her new book."

Finn frowned. "That sounds like a bad idea."

"That's what I thought. I feel like she is practically daring the killer to take action before she is able to make the big reveal."

"Do you know where she is staying?" Finn asked.

"She rented a house on the west shore, just north of Harthaven. It is the same house she rented when she met Amy when she was a child. Amy's family no longer lives in the house next door, and Winnie didn't mention an address, but I'm sure you can figure it out if you want to have a chat with her."

"I have the address in my file." Finn looked at Siobhan. "I hate to cut our evening short, but do you mind getting a ride home with Cait?"

"Happy to. If it turns out that you are going to be longer than an hour or two, text me to let me know what's going on."

Finn leaned forward and kissed his wife. "I will." He looked at me. "How long has Ms. Westminster been on the island?"

"I think she just arrived yesterday."

"And had you heard, prior to this evening, that the woman was claiming to have solved the Amy Anderson murder case?"

I shook my head. "No. I did know she had written a book based on Amy and her death, but until she said so this evening, I had no idea that she was actually identifying the killer."

"So maybe the killer hasn't heard that potentially dangerous information either."

I shrugged. "Maybe not. Unless the killer was at the meeting tonight or had attended one of the other bookstores along the prepublication tour. We've been advertising the fact that Winifred Westminster was going to be a guest at Coffee Cat Books for the past several weeks, and our ads did indicate that she had written a book about the Amy Anderson murder, and Winnie did indicate she either had made other stops or planned to make other stops before the book was published. Either way, if I was the killer and I still lived in the area, I might show up to hear what she had to say."

Finn narrowed his gaze. "I'll see if I can get Winifred to share what she knows for her own safety." He looked at Siobhan. "I'll call you after I get a feel for how things are going to go."

After Finn left, Tara, Siobhan, and I moved to a table. Aiden stayed behind the bar, but Danny joined us.

"I have to admit that Winnie's talk tonight brought up a lot of really weird emotions that I suppose I've been suppressing for years," Tara said.

"I know what you mean," I agreed. "The fact that Amy was murdered in a house filled with dozens of people and not a single person even knew she was dead until her body was found the next morning is beyond strange. It seems to me that she would have screamed if she was being attacked. If she did, you would think someone would have heard her."

"The music was loud that night," Danny pointed out.

"Maybe, but there must have been a struggle. It just seems unlikely to me that not a single person heard what was going on."

"I seem to remember that Amy was pretty drunk," Tara said. "Maybe she went upstairs and passed out. Someone could have killed her while she was out. She may not have even been aware of what was happening until it was too late to scream."

I picked up my wine and took a sip. "I suppose it could have happened that way." I knew Amy's body had been found on top of the bed in Lance Larson's parents' bedroom the morning after the party. The medical examiner had determined that she'd died at around eleven p.m., but apparently, no one had realized Amy was missing until the next day. "Does anyone remember how she died?"

"I remember reading in the newspaper that she was strangled," Danny answered.

"I wonder if Amy was drugged," Tara suggested. "If she had been drugged and then strangled, she might not even have fought back."

"I won't say I knew Amy well, but from what I did know of her, she didn't seem to be the sort to take drugs or drink until she passed out," I commented.

"She wasn't really herself that night," Danny said. "If you remember, Brock had just broken up with her, and he showed up at the party with Jamie."

Brock Stevenson had dated Amy all through high school, and I did remember that Amy took it hard when he broke up with her. Brock had brought a girl named Jamie Fisher to the party that night. Jamie and Amy were both popular cheerleaders, and most kids considered them to be rivals. "I remember that when Amy saw Jamie with Brock, she did not take it well, so I suppose that Brock showing up with Jamie might explain why she got so drunk, but it doesn't explain who killed her."

Siobhan had been listening, but she had already graduated and left the island by the time of the party, so she didn't really know any of the people we were discussing. When her phone buzzed, she picked it up and stepped away to take the call. Danny, Tara, and I continued to discuss possible suspects. Once we got to tossing around names, we came up with a fairly long list.

I glanced up as Siobhan returned to the table with a huge frown on her face. "What's wrong?"

"That was Finn. When he arrived at the house Winifred was renting, he found the front door partially open. When she didn't answer his knock, he let himself in. He found her dead on the living room floor."

"Dead?" I gasped.

Chapter 2

Siobhan nodded. "He said she'd been shot in the chest. He also said her death was recent. Very recent. He suspects the killer went out the back when he pulled up in the front. Finn wants you to compile a list of everyone you can think of who was both at the party on the night Amy died and, as far as you know, is on the island this evening."

"So Finn thinks that whoever killed Winnie also killed Amy?" Tara asked.

"It makes sense given the fact that Winnie announced to a room full of people that she knew who killed Amy and then she, herself, was killed shortly thereafter." Siobhan took out her phone. "I'll start a list. When we are done, I'll text it to Finn."

"Right off the top of my head, I'd start with Gavin and Brooke Prescott," I said. "Gavin was Amy's date on the night of the party. He'd dated Brooke Baxter all through high school, but apparently, on the night of the party, Gavin and Brooke were fighting and were considered to be on a time-out."

"I remember how angry Brooke was about it," Danny added.

"She had every right to be," Tara chimed in. "She'd been dating Gavin for more than three years; then they have one little spat, and he shows up at the homecoming party with another girl!"

"It was pretty rotten of Gavin to take Amy to the party, but Gavin and Brooke made up and are married with three adorable children, so it worked out in the end. I honestly don't think either of them killed Amy, but they were both at the party and are still living on the island, so in terms of means, it is possible."

Siobhan added both of them to her list.

"What about Brock Stevenson?" Tara said. "It is true that Brock was the one who broke up with Amy, and he brought Jamie to the party, but that didn't mean he wasn't jealous when she showed up with Gavin. And then she pretty much ignored Gavin and spent the entire night trying to get Chase Carter into bed, but I suppose Brock might still have been upset about the situation."

"Is Brock on the island?" Siobhan asked.

"Honestly, I don't know," I answered. "He shows up for homecoming every now and then."

"Perhaps we should have two lists," Siobhan suggested. "One can be for people who were at the party fifteen years ago, and we know, or have strong reason to believe, are currently on the island. Brooke and Gavin would be on that list. The second one can be for anyone who had a motive to want to hurt Amy and were at the party where she was killed but whose current whereabouts we are unsure of. Brock Stevenson would be on that list."

"What about Owen Nelson?" I asked. "I remember that he was at the party fifteen years ago, and he still lives on the island. I'm not sure he had a motive, but it still might be worth talking to him."

Siobhan added Owen to a third list, which she called Persons of Interest.

"And don't forget Lance Larson, if we are going to list people who may not have had a motive but still warrant taking to."

Lance Larson was the host of the party that night, and he was the one who found Amy dead in his parents' bed the next morning. He'd left the island after graduating high school, but his parents still owned the house where Amy died.

"It is reasonable to suspect that he could be in town for homecoming," Tara said. "I suppose we should at least check on his current whereabouts."

"I'll have Finn contact his parents," Siobhan said. "So, who else should we add to one of these three lists?"

"Lexi Michaels was at the party and also still lives on the island," Tara provided. "I have absolutely no reason to suspect that she would kill anyone, but she does fit the criteria of being in both places. In fact," she added, "Lexi was at the author talk tonight, so I know that she knew that Winnie was on the island and was claiming to have uncovered the identity of the killer."

"Lexi was Amy's best friend from elementary school," I pointed out. "There is no way she'd kill her, but she might know something that will help us figure out who did."

The four of us continued to discuss the possibilities until we'd compiled a pretty long list of those we knew for certain had both been at the party and still lived on the island, and those who had moved but it was reasonable to suspect could be back for a visit. Those who had moved and tended to visit, such as Lance and Brock, could be deleted from the list once Finn had confirmed they hadn't actually been on the island this evening. Danny needed to help Aiden close up, so we all agreed to pick up the conversation the following day.

Tara left in her own car, and I took Siobhan back to the estate, where she lived with Finn and their son, Connor, in the main house, and I lived with Cody in the beachfront cabin also on the property. We would move next door once the second and third floor of Mr. Parsons's house was renovated. The renovation was a major undertaking, but after Cody and I married and began to discuss living arrangements, we realized that it would be important to have a home to raise our family that we both felt ownership for. Mr. Parsons, the current owner of the home, lived on the first floor, while Cody and I planned to move into floors two and three. When Mr. Parsons passed, he planned to leave the entire estate to Cody and me.

"How is the work coming along?" Siobhan asked as we drove back toward the estate. "It looks like they have started the demolition from all the additional traffic on the peninsula."

"They just started, actually. We didn't want Mr. Parsons to be disturbed by the noise and mess, so we waited to get started until Balthazar got back from his trip." Balthazar was a man I'd met years ago and befriended. He lived in his own mansion by the sea and had invited Mr. Parsons to stay with him while renovations were underway.

"It was really nice of Balthazar to invite Mr. Parsons to stay with him."

I smiled. "Both men can be crotchety, that is for certain, but they seem to get along just fine. I think they will each enjoy the company of the other."

"Any idea when the remodel will be finished?" Siobhan asked.

"If all goes as planned, we should be able to move into the house in a couple of months. Three at the most. Why? Are you anxious to get rid of us?"

Siobhan laughed. "Not at all, but I know that Cassie is excited to have her own place. She is fine staying with Finn and me for now, but she is almost twenty-one, and she is excited to have her independence. You remember how it was when you first moved out of the family home where you grew up."

I did remember, and I had been even more anxious than Cassie to have my own place. "Speaking of Cassie turning twenty-one, we should talk about a party. Now that she'll be of age, I am thinking about asking the brothers if we can have it at the bar. They are closed on Mondays anyway, and Cassie's birthday is on Monday this year, so that part seems to work out."

"I think a party at the bar is a wonderful idea, although I think we should discuss our plans with Cassie before finalizing anything. I'd hate to plan something only to find out that she had something else in mind."

"I totally agree." I slowed to turn onto the Peninsula Road. "Cassie seems to enjoy hanging out with the family, but we should ask her. It is a milestone birthday. I can't believe she is going to be twenty-one. She has always been the baby of the family."

"And she always will be," Siobhan pointed out. "No matter how old you get, if you are the youngest, you stay the baby."

After I dropped Siobhan off at the main house, I took my dog, Max, for a walk along the beach. It was a dark night with a heavy cloud cover, but I had a flashlight, and Max and I didn't venture too far away from the cabin. While the house Cody and I were set to move into and would one day inherit from Mr. Parsons, was a fantastic one right on the sea, I had to admit that I was going to miss the little cabin where I'd lived since my aunt Maggie offered it to me when I was even younger than Cassie was now. It had been my home for a long time, and in many ways, it felt like an extension of myself. Cody and I planned to have a family, so the tiny cabin didn't make sense in the long run, but I knew that when I left it, I'd miss it a lot.

I loved these quiet walks along the beach with just Max and me. Not that I wasn't thrilled to have Cody join us when he was home, but it had been just Max and me for a number of years, and there was something special about spending one-on-one time with my furry best friend. I picked up a stick and tossed it down the beach, and Max gave chase. I glanced at my cell phone before slipping it into my pocket. I'd been expecting Cody to call this evening, but he never had. It was three hours later in Florida, so I doubted he would if he hadn't by now. I was disappointed that I hadn't heard from him, but I wasn't worried. Cody knew I had the author talk this evening, so he couldn't call me early in the evening, and his mother and uncle had been keeping him busy after dinner with the almost nightly bridge tournaments she entered with other members of her senior community. Cody wasn't one to really enjoy nightly card games, but he was a good sport and wanted to make his mother happy.

By the time I returned to the house, Cassie was pulling into the drive. I knew she had been at a party for one of her friends who was leaving the island. I waited for her to get out of her car.

"How was the party?" I asked.

"It was fun. Sad but fun. I've known Roxie since I was six. It is going to be so weird when I won't be able to call her to hang out whenever the mood strikes me."

"You couldn't hang out with her whenever the mood struck you when you were in college," I pointed out.

"True." Cassie slammed her car door. "But that felt different. For one thing, I was the one who left, while she was still here at home, where I felt like I needed her to be. And for another thing, I still saw her on weekends and during the summer. We were still able to make plans, but Roxie is moving to Texas. She is getting married and starting a new life. It really hit me that the odds are, I might very well never see her again."

I furrowed a brow. "You'll see her again. You can go visit her in Texas, or she can come back to Madrona Island for a visit."

"While I know that the possibility exists, I have to wonder if that is how it will work out. When my friend, Stephie, moved to Virginia two years ago, we promised we'd FaceTime every week and visit each other several times a year. We promised to stay in touch, but we didn't. We did FaceTime a few times in the beginning, but there was the time change to take into account, and she had her life, and I had mine. We really meant it when we promised not to lose touch, but losing touch is what happened anyway."

I supposed I understood what Cassie was saying. I'd had friends I'd been close to in high school who had left the island. We'd wanted to remain close, but in the end, once they'd moved, I'd never seen them again. There were a few who would show up for homecoming or class reunions, but as time went by, the frequency of those visits decreased. "Do you want to come in and have a glass of wine? You can tell me about the party, and I can tell you about the author who gave a talk at Coffee Cat Books and was murdered less than two hours later."

"Murdered?" Cassie looked skeptical. "Are you pulling my leg?"

"I'm afraid not."

"Winifred Westminster is dead?"

I nodded. "Shot in the chest. Finn is at the scene right now, trying to get a lead on who might have done it."

Cassie headed toward the side door of the cabin. "Isn't this the third death in the past few years that has been directly related to one of your book clubs?"

I paused to think about it. "Yes, I guess it is."

"You realize that the odds of being murdered after participating in one of your book clubs is going to cause people to think twice before attending?" Cassie hung her jacket on the coat rack near the door. She bent down to pet Max before adding that while she enjoyed working for Tara and me at Coffee Cat Books, she was beginning to think the job should come with hazard pay.

I headed to the kitchen and opened a bottle of wine. I poured two glasses and handed one to Cassie. "I guess I never stopped to think about the fact that we've had multiple deaths occur either at a book club meeting or immediately following one. It might be worth discussing the situation with Tara, although looking back, I don't think that attending our book club directly led to any of the deaths."

Cassie sat down at the small dining table next to the window that overlooked the sea. "That may be true about the other deaths, but if someone killed Winifred Westminster because of something presented in the talk she gave at the meeting, it sounds to me as if her death might very well be related to having attended your book club."

Dang if Cassie wasn't right. Although at this point there was a lot we didn't know.

"So, your birthday is on Monday," I said, changing the subject.

Cassie smiled. "Yes, I know."

"Siobhan and I talked about asking Danny and Aiden if we could use the bar that night for a private party so all your family and friends can celebrate with you. Is that something you would want us to do?"

Cassie took a sip of her wine before she answered. "Initially, I was thinking that I'd just skip having a party this year, but something small with family and close friends would be nice. Do you think we have time to invite Aunt Maggie and Michael? It wouldn't feel right to have a family event without them."

"I think we have time. They only live a ferry ride away. I'll call Maggie tomorrow. Mom too, and of course Marley. Why don't you make me a list of friends you want to invite and I'll take care of the family and family friends?"

"I'd like to invite Willow and Alex." Willow was a part-time employee at Coffee Cat Books, where Cassie worked full time these days. Cassie took another sip of her wine. "I'll go ahead and call the friends I want to invite. What time should I tell them?"

"Let's start at six. We can provide a dinner buffet and, of course, an open bar. I'll call the brothers and make sure it is okay to use the bar and that they have plenty of soft drinks for those who don't want alcohol. Once you get a head count for friends let me know, and Siobhan, Tara, and I will take care of a cake, and all the food."

Chapter 3

Wednesday, October 23

Cody would be home on the last ferry today, which had me excited. Saturday was the homecoming game and dance, Monday was Cassie's birthday party, and Thursday was Halloween. I'd called Mom and Maggie first thing this morning, and both assured me they'd be there for Cassie's party. It was convenient that Cassie's birthday fell on a Monday this year, and Coffee Cat Books was closed on Sundays and Mondays.

As for homecoming, Cody and I would be attending the game but planned to skip the dance. Danny and Aiden planned to have a homecoming reception at the bar, and Cody and I would be going to that. Finn hadn't come home until after I'd gone to bed last night, but his car was still in the drive this morning, so I grabbed a cup of coffee, and then head over to the main house to see if I could get an update on the Winifred Westminster murder case. When I arrived, Connor was sitting in his highchair eating pancakes, and Finn and Siobhan were sitting at the kitchen table sipping coffee. Cassie wasn't down yet, but she'd had a late night, so I wasn't surprised. I filled Siobhan in on my conversation with her about a party on Monday and then turned my attention to Finn. "So, did you figure anything out about the murder?"

"Not much. She was shot in the chest. Her body was still warm, and blood was still oozing from her body when I arrived, so it had just happened. I checked for a pulse, but there wasn't one. Based on the location of the entry wound, it appeared as if she'd been shot through the heart. I hadn't seen anyone nearby when I pulled up, so I am figuring the killer left through the back door and escaped through the wooded area at the back of the property. I didn't see any cars anywhere in the area, so I have to assume the killer either arrived on foot or left his or her car on the street on the far side of the woods."

"And the neighbors?" I asked.

"I spoke to everyone who lives both on the street where the house is located and the one beyond the woods area. No one admitted to seeing or hearing anything."

"How could the neighbors not have heard a gunshot?" Siobhan asked.

"It's possible the killer used a silencer," Finn answered. "I'm only just getting started with my investigation, so I hope I will be able to make some headway today."

"Did you find anything at all?" I asked. "Fingerprints, footprints, hairs, fibers, anything?"

"The crime scene guys had just arrived when I left to talk to the neighbors. When I returned from my interviews, they were still working, and I left to come home. I'm hoping they will have news for me today."

"The killer has to be someone related to Amy Anderson's death," I said with conviction. "I mean, I suppose it is possible that Winnie was simply the victim of something like a home invasion gone wrong, but really, what are the odds that will turn out to be the case?"

"I agree that Winnie most likely died because of what she had discovered about Amy's death," Finn said. "Siobhan gave me the list you made last night, so I have a place to start. If you think of anyone else who should be on the list, call me. I have a short list of people I remember being at the party who aren't on the list and whose whereabouts are not currently known. I'm going to see if I can track down the individuals who fall into that category."

"Like who?" I asked.

"Jamie Fisher, for one. I remember that she came to the party with Brock, creating quite a stir."

"Jamie moved to Florida years ago. As far as I know, she hasn't been back to the island since. She doesn't have the history with this place that some of us do; I don't think she moved here until sophomore year of high school, and she left shortly after graduation. I suppose that it's possible she could have killed Winnie, but I doubt it. I also really doubt she killed Amy. Sure, Amy hated her, and they did seem to have a rivalry of some sort going on, but Jamie was pretty indifferent to most people in general, and at the time of the party she'd only been with Brock for a short time. I didn't sense that they had any sort of deep, abiding love that would cause Jamie to act violently."

Finn made a few notes on the legal pad he was working from.

"What about Chase Carter?" he asked. "I was only at the party for a short while, but I seem to remember Amy hanging all over him."

I bit my lower lip. "The gang and I discussed the fact that Amy had been openly lusting over Chase at the party. I suppose he could be considered a suspect in Amy's death, but I have no reason to believe he is on the island now. You should probably try to ascertain his whereabouts, although in my opinion, his girlfriend at the time, Liza Tisdale, makes a more likely killer. She was so possessive, and she had this mean, jealous streak."

"And do we know if Liza is on the island?" Finn asked.

"As far as we know, she isn't, but again, it might be worth looking in to. I can think of a few others we might want to add to the list, but to be honest, I don't see any of these people strangling anyone."

"Amy wasn't strangled," Finn said.

I raised a brow. "Danny said the newspaper said Amy was strangled."

"The newspaper did say that, and as far as I know, Tripp let everyone believe that, but I took a look at the official medical examiner's report, and it said that Amy had been suffocated. There were no signs of strangulation."

Tripp Brimmer was the resident deputy at the time of Amy's death.

Siobhan got up and refilled everyone's coffee. "Don't you think it is too early to make the assumption that the person who killed Amy is the one who killed Winnie to the exclusion of all other possibilities?"

"I suppose it is early to eliminate all other possibilities completely," Finn said. "And I do plan to explore the option that there might have been someone who wanted Winnie dead for a reason totally unrelated to Amy Anderson. I don't personally think that is where we will find the killer, but I plan to spread a wide net at least in the beginning."

"If Winnie was killed because she found out who killed Amy, all we need to do is find out how her book ended," I pointed out. "I know she wasn't going to tell anyone how the story ended ahead of time, but the book was publishing in less than a month. Her editor and publisher must have the finished manuscript by now."

"Good point," Finn said. He stood up. "I'm going to head into the office and make some calls. If I can find someone who will send me the complete manuscript, I should be able to figure out who would want Winnie dead."

After Finn left, I went out to the cat sanctuary to feed the resident cats. Harthaven Cat Sanctuary was initially the love child of my aunt Maggie, but after she married and moved off the island, Siobhan, Cassie, and I took over the care of the cats. Taking care of so many cats was a big job, but now that Mayor Bradley had passed away and it was no longer legal to kill the feral cats that lived on the island, the number of animals at the sanctuary had decreased quite a bit. We did have cats surrendered to us from time to time, but I was usually able to get those in new, forever homes through the daily adoptions we did through Coffee Cat Books in a relatively short time. As I fed the cats, I was reminded of the fact that more often than not, if there was a murder to solve on the island, a cat would come along to help me with the investigation. This murder had only occurred last evening, but if tradition holds true, a cat would appear at some point today. Perhaps once I went into town for work, I would stop by to chat with my witch friend, Tansy. She acted as a guardian of sorts for the magical cats on the island, so if I had a feline helper on the way, chances were good that she would know about it.

Chapter 4

Tansy and Bella were friends who owned Herbalities, an island shop that specialized in herbal lotions and natural remedies. Each had special talents, which caused many to refer to them as witches, a title, by the way, neither had ever admitted to. I wasn't certain what title their talents should earn them instead, but what I did know was that Tansy had a way of seeing and knowing things that no one else seemed to be able to do.

When I arrived at the store, Bella was standing at the counter looking down at some sort of spreadsheet. "Good morning, Cait." Her bright blue eyes flashed with delight, and her waist-length blond hair was slipped over one shoulder.

"Good morning, Bella." I took in a deep breath. "Something smells heavenly."

"Tansy is trying out a new incense that is purported to aid in relaxation and stress release."

I took another deep breath in through my nose. "It does smell divine. I'm not sure it would relax me, but it does have a pleasant scent."

Bella smiled. "Tansy and I have come to the realization that while the incense *is* pleasant, it doesn't seem to have any specific medicinal value."

"Is Tansy here today?"

"She's upstairs. I'll get her. She has been expecting you to come by to ask about the recent murder."

"You heard about it?"

Bella tilted her head to the side just a bit. "We didn't hear anything, but Tansy knew. She is getting some things together for you to take with you."

I looked around the colorful and wonderful-smelling shop while I waited for Bella to fetch Tansy. When they had moved onto the island, I'd been fascinated by the mystical items they sold here, but after getting to know them, I'd learned that the women themselves were far more interesting than their wares.

"Cait," Tansy greeted me, gliding down the stairs. "You are just in time. Watson will be waiting."

"Watson?"

"The cat who has come to aid you in finding a killer." Tansy handed me a box. "Watson has been having some health issues, so you will need to add the supplements I am providing to his food twice a day."

"Health issues?"

"Don't worry. His health won't affect his ability to help you. He isn't contagious, so he can mingle with other cats, and in the long run, he will be fine. He understands what needs to be done and will guide you in your search for the truth. It's damp out today, and we don't want to leave him sitting on the dock for longer than need be, so it is best you run along."

"The dock?"

Tansy nodded. "Near the old boathouse. The one no one uses. Watson will be waiting near the entrance. Follow his lead, and you will find the answers you seek."

I thanked Tansy and left. I'd hoped to ask her a few more questions about what she might know about Winnie's death, but she seemed to want me to hurry, so I decided that was what I had better do. When I arrived at the dock, I found a beautiful brown cat waiting for me. He was thin based on his overall size, but I supposed that if he'd been ill, that would account for it.

"Watson, I presume?"

"Meow."

I bent down and scratched the longhaired cat beneath his chin. "I'm Cait. I guess we'll be working together for the next little while."

The cat began to purr loudly.

"I'm anxious to get started, but the past has shown that these things take time. I'm supposed to help out at the bookstore today. You're welcome to come along if that's okay."

The cat got up and trotted down the dock toward the bookstore, which seemed to indicate to me that he was just fine with my plan. As soon as we arrived, I let Watson in. I introduced him to Tara and Cassie before he trotted over and curled up on one of the sofas we provided for our customers. He fell asleep within minutes. The poor guy must be feeling the effects of his illness.

I glanced toward the cat lounge. Tansy had said that Watson wasn't contagious, so I decided to let him nap here at the store rather than taking him home.

"So this is a Tansy cat?" Cassie asked.

I nodded. "His name is Watson, and Tansy assures me that he will help me find Winnie's killer."

"Any news on that front?" Tara asked.

I filled them in on what Finn had shared with me that morning.

"We should have a Scooby meeting tonight," Cassie suggested.

"That's not a bad idea," I agreed. "Cody is coming in on the five o'clock ferry. I'll need to pick him up, but we can meet at the cabin at six."

"Six works for me," Cassie assured me.

"I'll pick up some takeout for dinner," Tara added.

"We should call to invite Finn and Siobhan," Cassie said. "Danny too, if he can get away from the bar."

After we briefly discussed who would call whom, I unpacked a box of new releases that had just come in while Tara and Cassie got the coffee bar ready for the first ferry of the day. During the summer, the bookstore tended to be busy all day, but during the off-season, the flow of customers more often correlated to the coming and going of the ferries that docked just across from our front door.

"Did you remember to order the Christmas decorations we talked about?" I asked Tara as I dusted the Halloween village we'd set up at the beginning of October. The villages Tara created for each season had become so popular, I knew that there were return customers who stopped by for no other reason than because they'd been enchanted by the tiny representations of a Halloween, Thanksgiving, or Christmas town.

"I did, including the ski lodge and the chairlift for the Christmas village," Tara answered.

"The haunted carousel has been a huge hit this month," Cassie informed us. "The haunted carnival was one of the most popular parts of the Halloween village last year, but now, with the carousel, it seems to have taken over as everyone's favorite. Not that the trick-or-treat village isn't still popular, especially with the younger kids."

"Are we still doing home by the sea for our Thanksgiving theme?" I asked Tara.

"We are. I have a new dock that is really awesome, but mostly, the scene will feature the same country homes as last year. Let's not forget to order the specialty syrups for both holidays. The pumpkin lattes and cinnamon teas are selling as well as always this month."

Deciding to move Watson to the cat lounge before the first ferry arrived, I picked him up, carried him into the adjoining room, and introduced him to the other three cats in attendance today. He sniffed them briefly, jumped up onto one of the sofas, and went back to sleep. I felt bad that the kitty was sick and hoped that he'd feel better soon, but I was concerned that trying to solve a murder with a sick cat as a helper was going to be pretty pointless. A lot of the cats I worked with didn't get started right away, so I supposed after the crowd from the first ferry cleared out, I'd take him home, introduce him to Max, give him his meds, and hope he'd be feeling better by the time I got home that evening.

When I returned to the coffee bar, Lexi Michaels was standing at the counter chatting with Tara, who was assembling a pumpkin latte.

"Morning, Cait," Lexi greeted me.

"Hi, Lexi."

"That was quite the presentation last night," she commented. "Did you know Winifred Westminster was going to tell everyone that she knew who'd killed Amy?"

I walked across the store and then sat down at the counter next to Lexi. "No. I knew she was working on a novel about Amy's death, but I had no idea that she was going to announce that she'd found the killer."

"The whole thing really hit me hard," Lexi said. "Amy was my best friend. We'd been close since the second grade. It took a lot of years for the pain of that night to fade into the background. I'm sorry that Amy died, and I wish I could go back in time and do something to change the outcome of the evening, but I can't, and to be honest, I really don't want to become bogged down in my memories again. I really hope this just blows over and we can get on with our lives."

"If Winnie actually identified the killer, that would be a good thing, wouldn't it?" I pointed out.

Lexi took a sip of her latte. "Perhaps. You know I wasn't even going to come to the book club last night, but Valerie Green wanted to, and she talked me into going with her. She even offered to drive and to treat me to pie and coffee after, so I agreed to satisfy my curiosity and see what Westminster had to say. Of course, now I wish I hadn't bothered. Amy's death seems to be the only thing I can think about today." Lexi paused and then continued. "Westminster didn't happen to tell you who she believed killed Amy, did she?"

"No. She didn't say." I wondered if I should mention that Winnie had been killed, but decided that I should talk to Finn about whether I should before I started spreading that interesting bit of gossip around.

Chapter 5

My spirits lifted immensely when Cody walked off the ferry and into my arms later in the day. He'd only been gone a little over a week, and I'd tried to stay busy, but God, I'd missed him. I could have gone with him to visit his family, but I had a bookstore to run and, quite honestly, after spending two weeks with them over Christmas last year, I'd found myself vowing never again.

"How was your trip?" I asked as Cody loaded his suitcase into the back seat of my car.

"Long. How were things here?"

I used that entry point to tell him about Winnie Westminster, her talk the previous evening, and her tragic death. "The gang is coming by tonight for a brainstorming session. I know you probably hoped we'd be alone, but this seemed important."

Cody reached across the seat and clasped my hand. He gave it a squeeze. "I did hope we'd be alone, but I understand. What time is everyone coming?"

"Six. Finn is bringing an update, Siobhan is bringing the whiteboard, Cassie is taking care of dessert, Tara is bringing takeout, Danny is bringing beer, and Mom and Gabe are babysitting Connor."

"It sounds like a family affair."

I smiled. "It is. The family that sleuths together stays together. I'm sure Aiden would have helped out if he wasn't needed at the bar."

"Did the new cocktail waitress start?" Danny and Aiden had lost the two they had when both had chosen to move off the island for different reasons.

"Not yet, but it's slow right now, so they're handling things. I think the woman they hired will be starting next week. Danny said something about her being there to help out for the Halloween Bash the brothers are planning."

Cody pulled onto the peninsula road. "I'm looking forward to Halloween. It was so hot in Florida. And muggy. It reminded me how much I appreciate the much cooler temperatures here on the island."

"I'm excited about the official kickoff to the holiday season as well. Our first as a married couple." I smiled at Cody. "Not only do we have the Halloween Bash on Thursday, but there is homecoming this Saturday and Cassie's birthday party on Monday. It will be a busy week."

Cody slowed as he approached the private road that led to the Hart estate. "It is going to be a busy week. I have a lot to do at the paper."

"I should have time to help if necessary."

"I want to be sure to cover the homecoming game this weekend. And I'd like to get some photos from the game to use with the article. The word around town is that our team has a good shot at winning the state title this year. If we do, it will be the first time in a very long time."

Cody pulled into the drive and got out. He took his suitcase in to unpack while I took Max out for a run. Watson seemed more interested in going upstairs to help Cody, so I left him behind. I supposed when I got back from walking Max, I should head over to the cat sanctuary to make sure that everyone was fed. Cassie had offered to bring the two cats that had not been adopted today home with her when she left the bookstore at around four, so she might have taken care of the feeding and cleaning as well.

I took in a deep breath as I followed Max down the beach. Like Cody, I loved the fall, with the colorful trees, crisp weather, and deserted beaches. I could hear the sound of seagulls flying overhead, but other than the sounds of nature, the beach was totally silent today. I felt lucky to live where I did. The peninsula was divided into three large estates. Francine Rivers owned the estate on the north end of the peninsula, Aunt Maggie had owned the estate in the middle until she'd married and given it to Finn and Siobhan, and Mr. Parsons, the man Cody had been living with for the past several years, owned the estate on the south end. Mr. Parsons would be leaving his estate to Cody and me in his will, and we planned to raise our family within the walls of that large home, so we'd begun to discuss the total remodel of the second and third floors after we'd married the previous fall. Things had been going well, and we hoped to be able to move in before Christmas, though at this point, having it ready in time was less than certain.

By the time Max and I got back from our walk, Cassie and Siobhan had arrived. Cassie assured me that she'd seen to the cats in the sanctuary, so I didn't need to worry about them. Siobhan assured me that Finn would be along shortly, and Danny had called to say he was on his way just as Tara pulled into the drive. Siobhan had already listed the names on the whiteboard that we'd written down the previous evening. I imagined that by the end of the evening, some names would be added while others would be crossed off.

"I picked up Chinese food. I hope that is okay with everyone," Tara announced as she began to unpack takeout bags and I set plates and utensils on the counter.

"Chinese sounds good to me," Cassie replied. "Did you get sweet and sour pork?"

"I did," Tara answered. "I picked up a lot of different things so everyone can mix and match. Is Danny coming?"

"He's on his way," I confirmed.

"Finn should be here at any time as well," Siobhan added.

By the time we had served ourselves, Finn and Danny had arrived. We chose to eat first and then jump into the discussion of Winnie's murder. Finn had indicated that he had news, but I supposed it was asking too much to hope that whatever it was had already cracked the case wide open.

After we'd all finished eating, Siobhan approached the whiteboard with a dry erase marker and Finn began to speak. "First of all," he said, "for the purposes of this discussion, I think we should entertain the idea that Winifred Westminster's death may be related to Amy Anderson's, but that the two are not necessarily connected. I feel it is too early in the investigation to limit ourselves to suspects who could have killed both Amy and Winifred."

Everyone agreed.

"Having said that, I'd like to begin by going over the motives and alibis of individuals who were on the island last night and at the homecoming party fifteen years ago."

Everyone nodded, indicating they were fine with that as well.

"I spoke to Gavin Prescott today," I informed the group. I'd decided to walk down to his office, which wasn't far from the bookstore when we'd experienced a lull in the afternoon. "If you remember, he attended the homecoming party as Amy's date after he broke up with Brooke and Brock broke up with her. Gavin told me that Brooke was spitting nails when he showed up at the party with Amy, but they talked it out afterward and, as you all know, they got back together and eventually married. They both still live on the island, but Gavin informed me that he and Brooke were both at the elementary school for their oldest daughter's choir recital until eight o'clock last night, and then they took all the kids out for ice cream, after which they drove home to put the kids to bed. I was able to confirm that the couple had, in fact, been at the recital with the school music teacher, so I think we can cross both of them off the Persons of Interest list as suspects in the Winifred Westminster case."

"What about the Amy Anderson case?" Tara asked.

"Gavin said that Brooke left the party shortly after he arrived with Amy," I informed the group.

"I remember Brooke getting mad and leaving as well," Finn joined in.

"Gavin was still at the party at the time the coroner determined Amy was dead, but he swears he didn't kill her," I jumped back in. "He said that when Amy started hanging all over Chase, he headed into the backyard to smoke pot with Brock and some other guys."

"I do remember seeing a group of guys smoking pot in the backyard," Danny agreed. "I can't swear that Gavin was with the group, but it doesn't seem as if he had any reason to kill Amy. Sure, he was her date, and she spent most of the night trying to get into Chase's pants, but despite the fact that they came to the party together, Gavin and Amy were never really a couple."

"I didn't know Brooke and Gavin well in high school, but I know them pretty well now, and I really don't see either of them as the sort to kill anyone," Tara added. "If they have an alibi for Winnie's death, I say we cross them off the list."

Everyone nodded.

"I spoke to Lexi Michaels today," I said. "She came to the author talk with Valerie Green. She told me the two of them went out for pie and coffee afterward. Given the timeline regarding Winnie's death, I don't think Lexi would have had time to go home, pick up her own car, drive up the coast to the rental where Winnie was staying, and shoot her."

Everyone agreed that we should take Lexi off the list as well, at least for Winnie's murder.

"Which brings us to Owen Nelson," Finn said. "I don't necessarily suspect Owen. He seems like a nice guy, and I really don't see that he had a motive to kill Amy, but he doesn't have an alibi for last night. He said he was home alone, and so far, I have been unable to verify that. I spoke to a few of his neighbors, hoping that someone saw him at home, but no one remembers if he was there or not."

"I guess for now we should leave him on the list," Siobhan said.

The others agreed; although I didn't think any of us suspected that Owen might actually be guilty.

"Did Owen know whether Archie or Becky had arrived on the island?" I asked.

"He said both are due to arrive tomorrow, which means they couldn't have killed Winifred, and I honestly don't see either of them killing Amy," Finn answered.

"Were you able to speak to Lance?" I asked. "Is he on the island?"

"I was unable to track him down, but according to his mother, he has been on the island since last Saturday," Finn answered. "Amy died in his house, so we have to assume he was around when Amy died. I say we add him to the Persons of Interest list, along with Owen."

Everyone agreed.

"Okay, so who else do we need to look at?" Cassie asked. She'd been a child at the time of the party, but I could see that she wanted to be part of the gang.

"We know that Brock Stevenson was at the party," Finn answered. "It has been suggested that he was in the backyard smoking pot with a group of guys, including Gavin, but he was Amy's ex, and I'm sure he must have had feelings about the fact that she was all over Chase. I tried to contact him today to see if he was on the island now, but he didn't answer his cell. I called his place of employment and was told he was on vacation. I don't know for certain that he is here on the island, but I think we should add him to the list."

The others agreed with this as well.

"We also know that Chase was at the party," Danny added. "I have not been able to track him down to find out whether he is currently on the island. My instinct is that he isn't, but I still think we should add him to the list until it can be confirmed one way or the other."

"Does anyone know whether Chase and Amy actually…" I paused. "I guess what I am asking is if Amy was successful in doing what it appeared she was trying to do with Chase. At the party."

"Cait wants to know if they had sex," Cassie clarified.

"I can't say for certain," Danny said.

We all felt that Chase should be added to the list at least until Finn could verify his current whereabouts.

"So that leaves who?" Tara asked.

"From my original list, that leaves Jamie Fisher and Liza Tisdale," Finn informed the group. "Jamie is not on the island, so I think we can cross her off at least in relation to Winifred's murder, but Liza is on the island visiting her sister, who has lived here the entire time. I have not had a chance to speak to her yet, but for now, she stays on the list."

Siobhan made the adjustments. "Okay, that leaves Owen Nelson, who doesn't have an alibi for the night Winifred died; Lance Larson, who is on the island, though Finn has not yet been able to speak to him; Brock Stevenson, who, according to his place of employment, is on vacation, although we don't know if that means he is here; Chase Carter, who was at the party, though Finn has been unable to track him down at this time; and Liza Tisdale, who had a motive to want Amy dead and is on the island visiting her sister, though Finn has been unable to speak to her so far. Anyone else?"

"I spoke to Tripp Brimmer today," Finn informed the group. "He told me that he had two strong suspects at the time of his initial investigation. Neither made our original list, but both are still on the island, so I think they should be added."

"And who is that?" I asked.

"Dalton Brown, for one."

"Coach Brown?" I asked.

Finn nodded. "According to Tripp, at the time of Amy's death, there had been a rumor circulating that she had been sleeping with him. Keep in mind that while Brown was a teacher, he was only twenty-four then, so that is not as surprising as it might initially seem. Still, Amy was seventeen and a minor when their dalliance allegedly began, so in Tripp's opinion, Brown had a motive."

"I suppose that if it came out that a teacher was sleeping with a student, he would have been fired at the very least," Cassie said.

"Was he at the party?" I asked, deepening my frown.

"He was there." Cody spoke for the first time since the meeting portion of the evening had begun. "He popped in for a short time. He had a couple of beers, chatted with a few members of his winning football team, and then left."

"But he could have slipped upstairs and killed Amy while he was there?" I asked.

Cody shrugged. "I suppose. It wasn't like I was keeping tabs on him. He showed up late. I would say it was around ten thirty or eleven. It seemed like he stayed for an hour or so."

"Was he with anyone?" Finn asked.

"Not that I remember," Cody said.

"He arrived alone but spent most of his time chatting with Chase and some of the guys," Danny added. "I do remember that he was there now, that his name has been brought up."

"Tripp said that he strongly suspected Brown but could never find the proof he needed to do anything about his suspicion."

"And the other suspect?" I asked. "You said Tripp had two."

"Dirk Gleason."

"I don't even remember seeing Dirk at the party. Hadn't he already left for college?" Tara asked. "He graduated the year before."

"According to Tripp, he was back for homecoming and showed up at the party late. One of the girls who was there told Tripp that he came in, grabbed a drink, and then headed upstairs. He didn't come downstairs until he left maybe thirty minutes later. She assumed he had shown up to talk to someone, but Tripp couldn't find anyone who would admit that they'd spent that half hour with him. Again, though, while Tripp strongly suspected him, he wasn't able to find any proof that he even knew that Amy was at the party."

"But he did speak to Dirk?" Danny asked.

"He did. Dirk told him that he had a private matter that he'd been there to tend to that had nothing to do with Amy and was absolutely none of his business. It was suggested that Dirk might have shown up to sell drugs. Tripp had verified that he had been busted for intent to solicit in the past."

Once we all took a minute to digest this information, Siobhan provided a summary of where we were, then asked what Finn wanted us to do next.

"I plan to try to track down Lance, Brock, Chase, and Liza tomorrow. I'm hoping that once I am able to chat with them, we will know whether or not they should remain on the list. It was late in the day when I spoke to Tripp, so I have not been able to follow up with Dirk Gleason or Coach Brown, but I will."

"I might be able to help you with Chase," Danny said. "We have some friends in common who might know how to get hold of him."

"And I'll pull the newspapers from around the time of Amy's death," Cody offered. "There might be a clue in either the articles or the notes Orson left that are associated with them."

"Did you ever get hold of Winnie's agent or publisher?" I asked Finn. It seemed to me that should probably have been the first question of this meeting because the odds were that one or both of them had seen the completed manuscript and could, therefore, tell us who Winnie had identified as Amy's killer.

"I spoke to Winifred's agent but was told that she wanted to keep the secret of who killed Amy Anderson to herself until the very last moment and had elected to self-publish this book. As far as the agent knew, no one other than Winifred knew how the book was going to end."

"Well, that's disappointing," I said.

"And it makes the fact that she was going around telling everyone that she knew who the killer was even more dangerous," Finn pointed out. "I'm very sorry that she was shot, but I think we can all imagine how she was setting herself up for exactly what happened."

"Should we meet again here tomorrow?" Cassie asked.

"I'm planning to head over to the bar in the afternoon to decorate for the events we have coming up during the course of the next eight days," Tara said. "I talked to Cait about helping me, and Willow is coming in to help you at the bookstore tomorrow. I will be free in the evening, however, if everyone else wants to meet."

"If we do meet tomorrow evening, let's do it at the big house," Siobhan suggested. "I can just put Connor to bed without having to get a babysitter that way."

Everyone agreed to the plan. I supposed we'd made progress today. We'd eliminated some names and added a couple others. I knew these investigations could take a while, but with everything we had going on and the holidays approaching, I really hoped we'd wrap things up sooner rather than later.

Chapter 6

Thursday, October 24

The sky was heavy with dark clouds the next morning. I hoped if a storm was going to blow in, it would do it today, do its thing, and then move out again before the big game on Saturday. The weather could be unpredictable during the month of October, so we'd need to be prepared for whatever Mother Nature delivered.

Cody had gotten up early and driven into town. As he'd mentioned the night before, he had a lot of work to catch up on today after having been out of town and wanted to get an early start. He'd taken Max with him, as he often did, so it was just Watson and me this morning. Tara had arranged to meet me at the bar at noon, and I'd considered heading into the bookstore before that, but it was early yet, so I had plenty of time to enjoy a cup of coffee and the view outside my window with my new furry friend.

"So, what do you think? Do you have any important information to pass along? I know you've only just arrived, and I know that while some of the cats who come here to help me jump right in, others like to take their time. I'm not sure how you feel about the timing of your involvement, but I am going to be at the bar for a good part of the day, so if you have a clue to lead me to, now would be a good time."

Watson just looked at me. The expression on his face made it appear that he was taking his time to think over the situation. Of course, I had no way of knowing what he was actually thinking or even if he'd understood what I'd been trying to tell him. One would think a cat wouldn't understand a word I said, but I knew from experience that Tansy's magical cats always seemed to understand exactly what I was trying to communicate.

After a couple of minutes, Watson jumped down from the chair he had been sitting on. He trotted across the room and batted a flyer off the coffee table. The flyer was advertising the book club talk on Tuesday, so at least I knew he understood why he was here and what I expected of him. I figured the only message he was trying to convey at this point was to confirm his understanding of the task at hand, but then he jumped up onto the coffee table, where the flyer had been left and sat directly on top of the old yearbook I'd been looking through after hearing that so many alumni planned to be in town for the homecoming game this year. The yearbook was from my senior year, so Amy would already have been dead for more than two years by the time it was published. I doubted that Watson wanted to show me anything in that book, but maybe Cody's yearbook, which would have photos of all the people we had discussed the previous evening, was what he was after. Taking a chance that I was on the right track, I called Cody and asked him if he knew where his yearbook might be. I suspected it was packed away with most of Cody's possessions, which were out of the way during the remodel, but if his wasn't handy, maybe Danny had his on hand. If nothing else, I supposed the high school library was an option, but that would be tricky. The library shelved yearbooks from every year since the school was open, but they couldn't be checked out, and I doubted the librarian would allow me to bring Watson inside to take a look.

Cody didn't answer my call, but it occurred to me that the yearbook from my sophomore year would be the same one that was published in Cody's senior year. I was pretty sure I had the yearbooks from all four of my years at Harthaven High School packed away somewhere; it was only my senior edition I kept close at hand. I paused to consider where I might have stashed the other three. Most of the memorabilia I had brought from home when I'd moved into the cabin was stored in the attic of the big house because the cabin had very little storage space.

"I need to run over to the main house to see if I can find the yearbook I assume you are looking for."

"Meow." The cat got up from the yearbook he was sitting on and shoved it onto the floor. Using a paw, he flipped it open. He pawed through the pages until he revealed a list of honor students.

"I don't understand what you are trying to show me. Is the clue actually in this book? You do know that Amy had already been dead for two and a half years by the time this book was published, right?"

"Meow."

I picked up the book and sat down on the sofa. I began to scan the list of students who had made the honor roll the year I graduated. I still wasn't sure the cat fully understood that this probably wasn't the yearbook we needed until I happened across the name of Lance Larson's younger sister, Lucy. "Lucy Larson. I forgot she was in my class." I looked at the cat. "Do you want me to talk to Lucy Larson?"

"Meow."

"But she wasn't at the party. She was out of town with her parents the night Amy died."

"Meow." The cat jumped onto my lap and began to purr.

Okay, I supposed I could try to speak to Lucy. She lived on Orcas Island, so unless she was planning to come to the homecoming game, I'd need to catch the ferry to make the short trip to the nearby island. It was nine fifteen now, and there was an inter-island ferry at ten thirty. If I hurried, I could make it to the dock in time. It would be a good idea to call Lucy to make sure she would be available to talk. She owned an arts and crafts shop in Eastsound that didn't open until ten. I didn't have her personal cell number, so I went upstairs to shower and dress, planning to call Lucy at her store before boarding the ferry.

By the time I took a quick shower, got dressed, and made the trip to the dock, it was a few minutes after ten. Cody had called back and left me a message letting me know that he'd noticed a missed call from me. I texted him back to let him know what I was doing and then popped into Coffee Cat Books to make my call to Lucy. As it turned out, she was at work and available to speak to me. She hadn't heard about Winifred and swore she didn't know anything about Amy's death, but if Watson thought she was a person of interest, it would be worth the short trip to the nearby island to find out what it was he was trying to tell me. The return ferry wouldn't get me back on Madrona Island until twelve forty, so I told Tara that I'd head over to the bar to help her decorate when I returned. She agreed to go ahead and get started, and I could join her when I could.

Living on an island, I took the ferry often. Depending on where I was going, I either brought my car or simply walked on. Today, I would need to drive from the ferry terminal to Eastsound, so I brought my car, which allowed me to bring Watson along for the ride. He seemed happy to curl up on the passenger seat and take a nap once we'd made our way onto the ferry and parked. I had no idea what it was Watson wanted me to discover, so I didn't know what I'd ask Lucy. I supposed that once we arrived at her shop, I'd simply initiate a conversation and see where it went. If Watson was correct and Lucy did know something important, hopefully, the subject would come up naturally.

Chapter 7

When I arrived at Lucy's shop with Watson, I found her standing behind the counter. I'd decided to put the cat on a leash because I wasn't sure how Lucy would feel about the feline wandering around her store. I didn't know how well Watson would do with the leash, but after a brief breaking-in period, he seemed to take to it just fine as long as I walked where he wanted me to go and didn't try to tug him in any other direction.

"Cait, how are you?" Lucy greeted me with an expression of confusion on her face. "I see you brought your cat."

"I hope that is okay. Watson is well behaved. He won't cause any problems."

"Okay." Lucy eyed the cat. She wasn't exactly scowling, but she didn't seem happy that I'd brought my furry friend along on the visit. "You mentioned on the phone that you had some questions about Amy Anderson's death."

I nodded. "I know you were out of town with your parents when Amy died, and to be honest, I'm not really sure what sort of information you might be able to provide that could lead to her killer, but I had a hunch I should speak to you, so here I am."

"You said that the reason you are looking into Amy's death again is because of the death of the woman who was on Madrona Island to publicize a book she had written about the murder."

"That's right. A true crime writer named Winifred Westminster spoke at a book club talk at Coffee Cat Books just an hour or two before she was shot. She told the group who attended the presentation that she had identified Amy's killer, so I am operating under the assumption that Winnie died because of what she figured out."

"Which is why you are trying to find out who killed Amy after all these years."

"Exactly."

Lucy leaned forward so that her forearms were resting on the counter in front of her. "Okay, I guess I understand what you are doing, but as you already said, I was not at the party, so I'm not sure I can answer any questions you might have. Have you spoken to Lance? He might be in a better position to help you with your research."

"Finn is going to speak to Lance." I paused and looked at Watson, who was watching us. Maybe I should have thought this through more thoroughly before I showed up. I had no idea how to even start. "I understand that Amy's body was found on your parents' bed the morning after the party."

"Yes, that is a well-known fact."

"Based on the determination of the medical examination, it appeared she died at around eleven p.m. That time of death seems to indicate that the party was still in full swing, so any number of people could have killed her."

Lucy nodded. "Yes. I suppose that is true, but that is also common knowledge. Are you going somewhere with this?"

Lord, I hoped so. "Your parents' bedroom is on the second floor at the end of the hallway."

"Yes."

"I remember Lance taped a note on the door letting everyone know the room was off-limits and would be locked all evening, which most likely explains why Amy wasn't found until the following day. I'm not sure how she was able to get into the room if it was locked, or why she wasn't seen going in by the folks who were lined up at the top of the stairs to use the bathroom."

Lucy just looked at me, as if waiting for me to get to the point.

"Is there another entrance to the room?" I finally asked.

Lucy nodded. "The bedroom has a private deck, and the deck has a ladder down to the backyard. If the sliding door between the bedroom and the deck was unlocked, I suppose that someone could have climbed up the ladder and gotten in that way."

"Climbed up the ladder. Are we talking about a steep ladder, like a fire escape?"

"Exactly like a fire escape. No one uses it, but my mom wanted a way to exit the second floor in addition to the regular staircase in case of a fire."

"Did Lance ever tell you why Amy was in the room?"

"Lance told the deputy that Amy hadn't been feeling well and that she asked if she could lie down. He let her into the bedroom and pulled the door closed behind him. He assumed she left the party at some point. It never occurred to him that she was still there when he went up to bed during the wee hours of the morning."

"So anyone could have let themselves in after Lance let Amy in."

"Lance said that the door was locked when he left Amy in the room. It is possible that she let someone in, but there was a long line down the hallway upstairs to use the bathroom, and he was sure that if Amy had let someone in the room, someone would have seen something. Lance was pretty sure that no one other than Amy went into the room. Of course, that couldn't be true unless Amy killed herself, could it?"

"No, I guess not." I chatted with Lucy a while longer and then said my goodbyes. Watson and I had some time to kill before the next ferry back to Madrona Island, so I grabbed some pastries from a local bakery and headed down to the beach. You could see Canada from this side of the island. It was a gorgeous view that I thoroughly enjoyed. While I was there, I noticed a yacht docked offshore. The water around the island was calm and tended to attract people looking for a weekend getaway, but the boat I saw in the distance looked to be larger than my cabin. I had to wonder which millionaire it belonged to.

By the time Watson and I made it back to the Orcas Island dock, the ferry had made the turn and was approaching. Once we arrived on Madrona Island, I stopped in at the store to check on Cassie and Willow. As soon as I entered with Watson, I was pleasantly surprised to see Becky Bollinger standing at the bar chatting with Cassie while she made her one of our specialty coffee drinks.

"Becky." I held out my arms in greeting. "How are you?"

"I'm fine. How are you?"

"Good. Really good. I heard that your software company has really taken off."

Becky nodded. "It's growing so fast, there are times I feel that I'll never be able to keep up with it, but I suppose that is better than the first couple of years when I really had to struggle to get a foothold." Cassie handed Becky her drink, and she stepped away from the counter and took several steps toward the door. "I'd love to catch up with you, but I have someone waiting for me in the marina."

"How long will you be in town?"

"Just for the weekend." She paused. "I heard about what happened to Winifred Westminster. I don't suppose you know who shot her?"

"No, I don't. Finn is looking into things, so hopefully, he'll have an answer soon. Did you know Winnie?"

"I wouldn't say I knew her, but I did talk to her. She called me at my office a couple of months ago wanting to ask about Amy. I agreed to talk to her, but I wish I hadn't."

"Oh, and why is that?"

"After asking a few very general questions about Amy and the night she died, she spent the rest of the time asking questions about Archie."

I frowned. "Archie? Why?"

"I don't know. She never really said, but she seemed to be trying to confirm something, or perhaps figure something out. I started off answering her questions, but then things got way too personal, so I cut the conversation short. She called back several times, but I wouldn't talk to her."

"Did it seem as if she suspected Archie of being involved in Amy's death?"

Becky took a sip of her drink before answering. "No. Her questions were more about Archie's work and personal life. She wanted details about what he did for the NSA, which I declined to provide. She asked questions about his home life and relationship status. As I already said, her questions really seemed to be geared toward finding out something about Archie that had nothing to do with solving Amy's murder, so I got off the phone and avoided her after that point. I talked to Owen about it, and he told me that she called him as well. As she did with me, she started off asking questions about Amy but then veered off in another direction and made the interview all about Archie."

"Did you tell Archie about her inquiries?"

"I did. He didn't seem overly concerned about it. He said that given the secrecy of his job, people are always interested in what he does for a living, but he didn't think either Owen or I knew anything that could hurt him even if we did spill the beans about what we knew. He also said he would talk to her personally and let her know in no uncertain terms that she'd best back off or suffer the consequences."

"What consequences?"

Becky shrugged. "He didn't say. Knowing Archie, if she didn't back off, he'd probably do something like hack into her bank account and transfer all her money to a charity supporting the preservation of garden snails."

"Garden snails need preserving?"

Becky chuckled. "No. I was kidding. Archie has an aberrant sense of humor, and while he is not the sort to get into a physical altercation, he can hack his way into pretty much anywhere and has been known to mess with people who mess with him by doing just that." She looked at her watch. "I really have to go, but maybe I'll see you at the homecoming game." She put her hand on the door and then paused. "Listen, if you find out what happened to Winifred Westminster, will you call me?"

"Sure. I can do that. Do you want to text me your number?"

After exchanging our contact information, Becky left the store heading toward the marina, and I went to the coffee counter. The fact that Winnie had called both Becky and Owen seemed relevant. Of course, at this point, I had no idea what any of it meant. Might Winnie have suspected Archie of killing Amy? I supposed it was possible, but I didn't see him as the killer. For one thing, I couldn't think of a single reason for him to have done so. He had been at the party, as had Becky and Owen, and it didn't make sense that any of them would have been there in the first place. It was too bad that Becky was in such a rush to meet up with whoever was waiting for her; I would have liked to ask her some questions about her memories of the night of the party. Maybe I'd run

into her at the game and could ask her then, or maybe
Owen knew what Winnie was really after.

Chapter 8

By the time I arrived at the bar, Danny and Tara were already busy with the decorations. I paused after entering the now empty space to watch them together. If I didn't know better, I would suspect the on-again, off-again couple was on their way to being on again. Tara hadn't said anything to indicate as much, but they had been spending a lot of time together lately, and since the breakup of Tara's relationship with her doctor boyfriend, they were both currently single. I wasn't sure how I felt about my brother and my best friend getting back together. I loved them both more than I could say and wanted them both to be happy, but they had tried the couple thing more than once in the past and on all of those occasions, their involvement had ended in heartache.

It didn't appear as if either of them had seen me come in. They were focused on posing a skeleton who was dressed in a football jersey with the number 21 stamped on it. The name on the jersey was Cassidy. I had to hand it to Tara; she'd managed to allow for the fact that the decorations would be used for the homecoming crowd, as well as Halloween and Cassie's birthday. The skeleton was posed so that it sat on the end of the bar. There was also a scarecrow wearing a football helmet sitting on a stack of hay bales, holding what looked like a birthday cake made from Styrofoam. The cake was iced in the school colors and, in honor of Cassie's birthday, it had the number 21 etched on the top.

"Wow, things are looking really good," I said, once I decided to stop lurking and continue into the bar.

Danny stood back to admire their handiwork. "Tara has come up with some excellent ideas to incorporate all three events O'Malley's will be hosting."

"I can see that. How can I help?"

"I have a box of rubber bats that need to be hung from the ceiling," Tara responded. "We'll want several over the bar, but the rest can just be distributed around the bar."

"Where's the ladder?" I asked.

"I'll get it," Danny said. "I was using it for the fake cobwebs in the hallway."

"So, how was your trip to Orcas Island?" Tara asked after Danny went for the ladder.

"Lucy was out of town with her parents when Amy died, so I didn't expect her to know a lot, but she did provide one piece of interesting information."

"And what was that?"

"Do you remember that Lance locked the door of his parents' bedroom? He put up a 'stay-out' sign and told everyone that the room was off-limits during the party."

Tara nodded. "I remember that. At one point there was almost a riot over the fact that there was a third bathroom in his parents' master suite that would make the wait time a lot more tolerable if Lance would just unlock the door and let the guests use it."

I'd sort of forgotten that, but Tara was right. There *had been* partygoers asking to be let in to use that third bathroom. "But Lance told everyone no," I responded. "He insisted the entire night that his parents' bedroom was off-limits. It occurred to me to ask myself, given the situation, how Amy got in there to pass out on the bed in the first place."

Tara raised a brow. "Good question."

"Lucy told me that Amy wasn't feeling well, so Lance let her in, but he locked the door when he left her so that no one else would be able to get in the room. Lance didn't think that Amy had let anyone else in, but she must have. There was a long line for the bathroom, so someone must have seen who Amy let in."

"So whoever Amy let into the room must have been the killer."

"Unless Lance was the killer," I countered.

Tara frowned. Danny must have heard my comment as he returned with the ladder because he asked me why I thought Lance might be the killer. I shared with him the information I'd just told Tara.

"I can't think of a single reason that Lance might want to kill Amy, but it does fit that he could be the killer," Danny said. "If he killed her at around eleven o'clock, it would also explain why he was so steadfast in his determination that no one could go into the room even after half the guys at the party started using his mother's flower bed as a urinal when the line for the bathroom got too long."

I wrinkled my nose. "Ew. Guys are disgusting."

Danny chuckled. "I seem to remember a female or two out in the yard too once the beer started flowing."

"Can we change the subject?" Tara said.

"Please," I agreed. "I stopped by the bookstore on my way back from Orcas and ran into Becky."

Tara smiled. "I hoped she'd make it here this weekend. How is she?"

"She was in a hurry to meet someone, but she did tell me that Winnie called both her and Owen. She said that after asking a few questions about Amy, she spent the rest of the conversation asking about Archie."

"Why was Winnie asking about Archie?" Tara asked.

"Becky wasn't sure. She said it seemed as if she wanted to either confirm something she thought she knew or discover something she didn't know but wanted to."

"I spoke to Gavin this morning, and he told me that Winifred called and asked him a bunch of questions a while back as well," Danny informed us. "He didn't mention Archie, but it seems that she has been digging around in the lives of anyone I imagine she considered to be a suspect."

"Why would Archie, Becky, or Owen be suspects?" I asked.

We all agreed that none of the three were likely suspects in Amy's death, so it made no sense that Winnie had called and spoken to them. She hadn't called Tara, Danny, Cody, or me, and we'd all been at the party, just as Becky, Archie, and Owen were.

"So what do we really think about Lance as the killer?" I asked, bringing the conversation back around to the point where it had veered away from our own suspect list. "He was the only one with access to the bedroom where Amy's body was found."

"The fact that Lance is the only one who seemed to have had the opportunity to kill Amy does point to his guilt," Danny said. "But what about motive?"

"Finn planned to track down Lance today, so hopefully, he will have the chance to ask him some of these questions. I guess all we can do right now is bring up our information and questions at tonight's meeting and see what the others think. Maybe Cody or Finn remember something that we don't from that night." I looked at Danny. "You were going to try to track down Chase. Did you ever get in touch with him?"

"Not yet. I have some feelers out, but so far, no one I've spoken to has talked to the guy in years. I'll keep asking around if Finn isn't able to locate him."

I grabbed the ladder and the box of rubber bats and began to hang them from the string I had been provided. Tara and Danny continued to discuss Chase and the likelihood that he had been the one to silence Amy after having been lured to the bedroom, but I didn't think he'd turn out to be our guy. In terms of means, I supposed that Lance topped the list, but in terms of motive, I could think of at least five other partygoers who would have had much more of a reason to want Amy dead.

"Do you think we should put up some streamers or will they be too much?" Tara asked.

I looked around the room. Between the bats and cobwebs, I didn't think we needed anything else hanging from the ceiling and told her as much. I glanced around the bar for Watson because it occurred to me that I'd become distracted and hadn't been keeping an eye on him. I found him happily stalking one of the bats that had somehow fallen to the floor. He was a beautiful cat, and I enjoyed his playful energy now that he'd begun to settle in. Hopefully, the supplements Tansy had given me to add to his food would do the trick, and he would be restored to his full health in no time.

"We need to get a picture of this place once we finish," Tara said. "It is turning out even better than I envisioned."

"I got a new phone that will take a panoramic photo," Danny offered. "If we can get a good enough shot, I'll upload it to O'Malley's Facebook page."

"I wonder if our skeleton needs a hat," Tara said.

"I have a baseball hat in the team colors, but we are celebrating a football game, so I think the jersey is enough," Danny answered. "Still, it wouldn't hurt to take photos with and without the hat to see how they look."

"You know, checking out photos isn't a bad idea," I said. "Do either of you remember if anyone was taking photos on the night of the party?"

"I'm sure Owen was," Tara said. "He used to take photos of everything."

Tara was right. Owen *did* take photos of everything. It might make sense to stop by to have a chat with him. I decided to ask Cody if he could watch Watson while I went. Maybe Owen had captured something that would explain exactly what had happened even if he hadn't been aware of it at the time. A quick call to Cody informed me that he would be happy to keep an eye on Watson. He also shared that he'd been able to pull the hard copies of the newspapers printed around the time of Amy's death from the stash in the morgue. While Orson had never attempted to offer a suggestion about who might have killed the teenager, he did indicate that, based on interviews he'd conducted, he felt there might be more going on than met the eye. Unfortunately, he hadn't been specific as to what he meant by that. Cody was going to do some digging to see if he could find any notes or drafts that Orson might have left behind.

Chapter 9

The photography studio Owen owned was in Harthaven, near the marina. I dropped off Watson at the newspaper so he could hang out with Cody and Max and then headed in that direction. I hadn't known Owen all that well when we were in high school; he was two years older than me and not the sort to hang out with the crowd Danny did. But since we were both adults, our paths had crossed on numerous occasions, and I found him to be an open and honest guy.

"Hey, Cait. I take it you are here about the photo we discussed for your new home?"

"Actually, that isn't why I'm here. You might have heard about the death of the author who was on the island to promote her novel based on Amy Anderson's death."

"I did hear that. It's tragic really, but I suppose by telling everyone that she had identified the killer and then refusing to tell anyone who she thought it was, she was asking for trouble."

"I agree. The way she approached things was not a good idea. Listen, the reason I'm here is because I ran into Becky today, and she mentioned that Winnie Westminster had called you to ask questions about Amy's death."

Owen bobbed his head. "That was the reason she gave for the phone call in the first place, but the reality was, she seemed more interested in asking me about other people than she was in asking me about Amy."

"Other people? Like who?"

"Becky, Archie, Lance, and Chase, mostly. I suppose I could understand why she might be taking a look at pretty much everyone who was at the party, but her questions seemed geared toward digging up dirt on the individuals on that list."

"Becky mentioned that she had a similar experience. Do you have any idea what she was really after?"

"No idea at all. If I had to guess, she was looking for something specific. I probably should have talked to her longer in an effort to figure it out, but I wasn't in the mood to be pumped for information about the private lives of my friends."

"Can you remember any of the questions she asked?"

"She knew that Archie worked for the NSA, and she was curious about exactly what he did there. I told her it was classified, and anyway, I didn't know. She also asked about the relationship status between Becky and Archie, which I told her was none of her business. And she wanted to look at any photos I had taken on the night of the party, but I told her I hadn't taken any and left it at that."

"Had you taken any, though?"

Owen shrugged. "I did, but I wasn't going to show them to that nosy woman."

"I get that, but after speaking to several people who attended the party, there seems to be a variation in the way people remember things. I hoped that photos might shed some light on these different interpretations. Would it be too much trouble for me to see what you have? When you have the time, of course."

Owen nodded. "Sure, I would do that for you. I have plans this evening with Archie and Becky, so it will have to wait until tomorrow. Actually, I'm not sure I'll even be able to get to it tomorrow. I'll be working during the day, and then a group of us are going out on Chase Carter's boat in the evening."

So Chase *was* in town. "I wasn't aware Chase was on the island."

"He's not. I mean he is, but he's not," Owen corrected himself.

I raised a brow.

"What I mean is that Chase owns a yacht that is anchored offshore. I don't think he has come ashore yet, but Becky is with him, and she told me they both plan to attend the homecoming game on Saturday. In the meantime, they invited Archie and me to dinner tomorrow evening. He's sending a shuttle to take us out to the boat."

"Is his vessel that huge yacht offshore? I noticed it when I was on Orcas Island earlier today."

"That would be it. The yacht is the size of a house from what Becky told me."

"I wasn't aware that Becky and Chase were friends."

Owen lifted a shoulder. "They weren't in high school. In fact, socially speaking, they were about as far apart as two people in the same graduating class could be. But I guess Chase hired Becky a while back to design a marketing and distribution system for the chain of sporting goods stores he owns. They worked closely together on the design, and according to Becky, they really hit it off. Becky told me they've been dating for the past six months or so."

Well, what do you know about that? The class nerd and the class jock had found common ground as adults. "That's really great. Becky mentioned that her software company has really taken off, and it sounds like Chase is doing well. I'm looking forward to catching up with both of them at the game. Will you be coming to the after-party at the bar?"

"I'd planned on it. I mentioned it to Archie, but he was less enthusiastic about the idea. I plan to work on getting him to consider it."

"Why wouldn't Archie want to come and hang out with everyone?" I asked.

"Your brother and his friends tended to pick on Archie and me when we were in high school. In fact, we were kicked out of the party where Amy died before it even really got going."

"Kicked out? Why?"

"According to Lance, Danny, and some other guys from the football team, we hadn't been invited."

I frowned. "I'm sorry. I wasn't aware that you weren't allowed to stay. I do seem to remember that you left early, but I didn't know why." I narrowed my gaze. "If you weren't invited, though, why did you show up?"

"I didn't want to. Becky either. But Archie had a crush on some girl he'd heard was going to be there and insisted we stop by, invited or not."

"What girl?"

Owen shrugged. "He never did say. I thought it might have been Lexi Michaels because I had seen the two of them together a few times, but he insisted that he and Lexi were just friends and he had no romantic interest in her."

"Lexi was friends with Archie?"

Owen shrugged. "Apparently. I guess they had biology together, and he was tutoring her or something like that. Anyway, the point of this story is that back in high school none of us were fans of Lance or Danny or really any of the A-list crowd, so it makes sense that Archie would be less than thrilled to show up at a party hosted by one of the guys who picked on him all those years. As I said before, though, I'm going to work on him to see if I can get him to reconsider."

"Please do. And I'm sorry about the way you were treated." I turned to leave. "By the way, do you know when Archie arrived on the island?"

"Wednesday. He plans to stay through Sunday."

After I left Owen's place, I went back to the bar. It seemed as if Danny and Tara had a handle on the decorations, but I had offered to help out, so I should check in with them one more time before I called it quits for the day. After all, I really hadn't helped out at all other than to hang a few bats. When I arrived at the bar, Danny and Tara were arranging fall garland around the bar.

"How'd it go with Owen?" Danny asked.

"He said that you and some of the other guys kicked him out shortly after he arrived at the party."

At least Danny looked somewhat sheepish in response to my statement. "Yeah, I guess we did kick out Owen and his friends, but in my defense, they had not been invited. I guess if you are going to crash a party, you should expect to get kicked out."

"Owen was in your class," Tara reminded Danny. "It was a party to celebrate the fact that the football team clobbered the opposition in the homecoming game. It was mean to kick out Owen and the others."

"Maybe it was mean to kick them out, but it was rude to show up at a party you had not been invited to. Besides, it was Lance's party, and he was the one who decided to limit the invites to his friends and their guests."

"Tara and I weren't invited, and you didn't kick us out," I pointed out.

Danny laughed. "I wanted to, and I even suggested to Lance that we do so, but Cody stepped in and told Lance that the two of you were with him."

Ah. That was sweet of him. I married a good guy, but apparently, my brother was a jerk. "So, if you kicked out Owen, Archie, and Becky, none of them could have killed Amy."

"I guess that is true," Danny admitted. He frowned. "Although I do remember seeing Archie later in the evening. Maybe he came back, or perhaps he never actually left. Either way, it was rude of us to kick them out, and I will apologize to them when I see them."

"Thank you. That would be nice. I suppose we all did things in high school we aren't proud of."

"Some of us more than others." Danny chuckled.

"Did you know that Becky is dating Chase now?" I asked.

Danny's brows raised in surprise. "Really? I hadn't heard. It's hard to imagine the two of them together. Chase was on his way to the top when he left Madrona Island and Becky, while smart, never seemed to put all that much effort into her appearance. I'm surprised Chase would go for someone like that."

"Someone like that?" Tara punched Danny in the arm.

"Ouch. That hurt."

"Good, it was supposed to hurt." Tara looked downright angry. "I don't know Becky all that well, but from what I remember and what I can tell based on what I have heard, she is not only smart, but she is driven and business savvy as well. Chase, or anyone for that matter, should consider themselves lucky to spend time with someone like Becky."

"Tara is right," I added. "And while guys like you and Chase might have been all that in high school, that's long over, and I think it will do you well to remember that you are no longer the big guy on campus. You own half a bar and Becky owns a multimillion-dollar software company."

Danny raised his hands in a show of surrender. "Hey, I'm sorry. I didn't mean to hit a nerve. I was just trying to point out that Chase and Becky don't make a likely couple."

I'd actually had the same thought but didn't want to admit it. Instead, I let out a loud huff and headed toward the door. If Danny wanted his bar decorated, he could do it himself, the big jerk.

After leaving the bar, I headed toward the newspaper to check in with my wonderful husband. It warmed my heart to hear that he'd vouched for Tara and me when my own brother wanted to have us kicked out of a party we'd admittedly crashed. I supposed that it wasn't abnormal for brothers to treat their little sisters that way, but it still teed me off to no end.

When I arrived, I found Finn chatting with Cody.

"How'd it go with Owen?" Cody asked.

"It went fine." I crossed the room and kissed Cody on the lips. "Thank you for being such a good guy even when my brother was a total jerk."

Cody looked confused.

"I'm sensing a story," Finn said.

I filled both men in on my conversations with both Owen and Danny, which had Finn chuckling.

"It's not funny. I'm pretty mad," I said.

"I can see that," Finn responded. "However, if we can verify that Owen, Archie, and Becky left the party before Amy went upstairs, that gets them off the hook for Amy's murder, and it sounds like Archie and Becky weren't even on the island when Winifred was killed."

"I remember Danny and Lance kicking the others out," Cody said. "I tried to talk them into letting them stay, but they were adamant that admission to the party was by invitation only. It seems to me that they arrived at around nine and were escorted out shortly after."

"It sounds like we can take them off the list," Finn said. "Not that any of the three were serious suspects anyway. I would like to speak to all three of them, however. You never know when someone might have seen or heard something that might not seem significant to them but actually turns out to be just the clue needed to solve the case."

"It sounded like Chase and Becky weren't planning to come to the island until tomorrow, but I ran into Becky at the bookstore earlier, so I guess she changed her mind. Owen confirmed that Archie is here on the island, so you should be able to can track him down. I'm sure Owen knows where he is staying."

"I'll stop by to ask Owen about Archie. I wanted to talk to him anyway."

"Were you able to connect with any of the others?" I asked.

"I spoke to Brock. He is on vacation in Hawaii, so he couldn't have killed Winifred. I have an appointment to meet with Liza this afternoon, and I hope to see Owen and then Archie after that."

"Were you able to talk to Dirk Gleason or Coach Brown?"

"I have messages in with both and am hoping to hear back from them today."

"I spoke to Lucy Larson today," I informed Finn.

I filled him in on what she'd said about access to the room and how that lined up with my recollection of the evening. Finn admitted that accessibility was something to consider, but it was also possible that someone could have climbed the ladder, gotten into the room, and unlocked the door at some point. I'd hoped we'd be narrowing in on the killer by this point, but in a way, I felt as confused as I'd ever been.

Chapter 10

Friday, October 25

Watson seemed restless the next morning. Cody had left for the newspaper early again, and I'd hoped to sleep in a bit, but after the third time the cat pounced on my head, I decided to get up. The weather had been unpredictable the past few days, raining one minute and then sunny the next, but so far today looked as if it was going to shape up to be a wonderful day, with the sky as blue as the sea.

"Okay, so what's the deal?" I asked Watson after I'd made my way downstairs and poured a cup of coffee.

"Meow." Watson jumped up on the counter and began to paw at the newspaper Cody had brought home the previous evening.

"You want me to see something in the newspaper?"

"Meow."

I set down my coffee cup and opened the paper to the first page. Watson just looked at me. I turned the pages one at a time until he let out a long howl when I opened to pages six and seven. I looked down at the open newspaper in front of me. There were quite a few ads on these pages, as well as a story about the upcoming homecoming game and a mention of a fund-raiser for new cheerleading uniforms. There was also a mention of the annual haunted house sponsored by the community, as well as a reminder to keep porch lights lit until all the trick-or-treaters made it home.

"So, what am I looking at?" I asked.

Watson placed his paw on an ad for the local bakery.

"You want me to go to the bakery?"

"Meow."

I raised a brow. "I'm not sure cats are supposed to eat doughnuts."

Watson jumped down from the counter and headed to the door.

"Okay, we'll go to the bakery, but I need to get dressed first. Give me a couple of minutes."

Watson began to paw at the door. I could see that he was in a hurry, but there was no way I was going into town wearing my pj's. I figured I would shower later to save time. I pulled on some old sweatpants and a sweatshirt, ran a comb through my hair, and slipped flip-flops on my feet. I then grabbed my purse and headed out to the drive with both Watson and Max on my heels. I let the animals in the back and drove toward the bakeshop, hoping all the while that I wouldn't run into anyone I knew. Generally speaking, my hair didn't look good after I'd just rolled out of bed and I realized after I was halfway to town that the sweatshirt I'd pulled on had a jelly stain on the front.

Of course, as luck would have it, I ran into a group of my old classmates who were having coffee and were just getting ready to leave the bakery when I arrived. The four women were in town for the homecoming game, so I had to stop to chat for a minute.

"It seems like the turnout this year is the best it has been for a long time," one of the women said.

"I have run into a lot of alumni, although I feel like there are more folks in town from Danny and Cody's class than ours," I said.

"I ran into Brooke Baxter yesterday," another of the women said. "Although I guess she is Brooke Prescott now, isn't she? I always figured Brooke and Gavin would end up together even after they broke up during their senior year." She grinned at me. "What I never saw coming was you and Cody West. Congratulations, by the way."

"Thank you." I grinned. Sometimes even I couldn't believe that little Caitlin Hart had ended up marrying Cody West.

"I ran into Chase Carter with Becky Bollinger when we were at dinner last night," one of the other women said. "Talk about an even more unlikely couple than you and Cody."

"I'd heard they were dating," I replied.

"I hear Becky is some sort of a millionaire many times over," someone said. "I always knew she would go places, but I had no idea she would do as well as she has. I guess it is hard to tell how a person will turn out based on their social presence in high school alone."

"I was even more surprised to find out that Chase owned a chain of sporting goods stores," another commented. "I always took him for just a dumb jock, but I guess my impression was wrong. I read somewhere that he had been named one of the forty under forty to keep an eye on. Not that keeping an eye on him was ever any sort of hardship. He is and always has been gorgeous."

He was at that, I had to agree.

"Speaking of people who have done well for themselves, I understand that you opened a bookstore with Tara O'Brian," one of the women said.

I nodded, although I didn't think that Tara and I were in quite the same category as Chase and Becky. "Coffee Cat Books. You should stop by while you are on the island. It is right across the wharf from the ferry terminal."

"I saw it when we arrived but wasn't aware that you owned it then. Now that I know you do, I will be sure to check it out."

"I'm enjoying catching up with everyone," someone said. "I ran into Archie Baldwin on Tuesday, and I saw Lexi Michaels at the farmers market on Wednesday. I am heading to Harthaven today, so perhaps I'll stop in to visit with a few of the others who stayed on the island."

"You ran into Archie on Tuesday?" I asked.

She nodded. "I guess I shouldn't say I ran into him exactly. I was sitting at the stoplight on Main and Second, and he pulled up in his Lamborghini. He's changed a lot, but I knew it was him because of the Lamborghini. He posted a photo of it on his Facebook page when he bought it last summer. It's a beautiful car, but I'm not sure about the color."

"Color?" I asked.

"Lime green."

I wrinkled my nose. I didn't suppose that was a color I would choose either. "Did you speak to him?"

"I rolled down my window and said hi. He said hi back. I reminded him who I was, and then the light changed. He waved one more time and then took off at a speed my little Subaru was never going to keep up with. I haven't run into him since, but I guess he'll be at the game tomorrow. I'm hoping to have a chance to ask him about his work. I hear that he has some sort of a top-secret government job building weapons or spying on foreign countries or something."

"No," one of the others said, "I think he works for the CIA doing counterintelligence."

"I'm pretty sure he was working with weapons and high-tech communications systems," a third woman joined in.

I decided to jump in. "Archie works for the NSA. I'm not sure what his job entails exactly." I paused to let the idea that Archie had been on the island on Tuesday roll around in my mind. Owen had assured me he hadn't arrived until Wednesday. Of course, Archie could simply have come early and failed to mention it to Owen. Still, it seemed like something I ought to store away in my brain.

I chatted with the women for a few more minutes and then returned to the car, where Watson and Max were waiting. I never did get around to buying anything in the bakery, but I didn't think that was what Watson had been after. "Okay, so I ran into some old classmates who informed me that Archie was on the island on Tuesday. Is that what you wanted me to know?"

Watson began to purr.

"Is Archie involved in the murders in some way?"

"Meow."

I paused to think about it some more. "Owen told me that he, Archie, and Becky had been kicked out of the party shortly after they arrived. Danny confirmed that, so it doesn't seem as if Archie or any of the others from that group could have killed Amy."

"Meow."

It seemed as if Watson agreed with this. "So, why do I need to know that Archie arrived on Tuesday rather than Wednesday?"

Watson didn't reply. Of course, he was just a cat, so it wasn't as if he could explain it to me.

"Okay. I guess I'll need to wait to see where this fits in. Is it okay to go home so I can shower now?"

"Meow."

When I got home, I called Tara to let her know I'd be late for work. She told me to take my time because both Cassie and Willow were coming in this morning. Then I texted Cassie and Siobhan to make sure that one of them had seen to the cats in the sanctuary. Cassie assured me that she had fed the cats and picked out three to take to the store that day. I mentioned that I'd be late, so she offered to take the cats in with her. It was working out really well that Cassie was here to help both Siobhan and me. I hadn't been thrilled when she'd told me that she wouldn't be returning to college this year, but she seemed to know what she wanted and what she didn't, and what she didn't was to be away from the island. I hadn't gone to college, and I felt things had worked out just fine for me, so I supposed I really shouldn't have anything to say about her decision not to continue when I'd never even tried it.

I showered and dressed for the day, then took Max for a run down the beach before heading into work. Cody was visiting some of the local advertisers this morning, so he hadn't taken Max into work with him, but he'd promised that he would come by to pick him up later after he'd finished his sales calls. I wasn't sure what to do with Watson today. I supposed Cody wouldn't mind taking him into the paper as well. I'd call him later and talk to him about it.

"It looks like someone found time to carve jack-o'-lanterns," I said to Tara when I walked into Coffee Cat Books to find several on the counter.

"I had a lot of pent-up energy after I got home from the bar last night. I had a bunch of pumpkins to carve, so I decided to do some now and some closer to Halloween."

"I take it your pent-up energy had something to do with the spat you had with Danny yesterday."

Tara shrugged. "I guess it did, although I guess I wouldn't say Danny and I had a spat exactly. It's just that I knew Danny in high school, I knew how he was, but I also know he has matured and changed. I guess his attitude about Becky just hit me wrong."

"Yeah, me too. Although if I am honest and someone told me that the most popular girl in high school was dating the nerdiest guy, I would have a similar reaction, so the fact that Danny's initial impression that the most popular guy was dating the nerdiest girl can be understood."

"I hate that word. Nerd. What does it even mean?"

"I think it means that someone is smart, which shouldn't be a bad thing," Cassie answered. "In fact, it seems that being a nerd is trendy these days, and guys like Archie are almost more popular than jocks. I guess we can thank the advances of technology for that."

Tara poured water into the coffee machine. "I suppose that is true to some extent." She added coffee grounds. "So, did you tell Finn that Archie was on the island on Tuesday and technically could have killed Winnie?"

"Not yet, but I will. Archie seemed to have already left the party by the time Amy was murdered, so I don't consider him a suspect, although Danny did say he thought he saw him later in the evening. Still, I really doubt he did it, and if he didn't kill Amy, he wouldn't have had any reason to kill Winnie, which means the fact that he was on the island a day earlier than Owen thought probably is not all that important."

"If it is not important, why did your magical kitty drag you into town so early this morning?" Tara asked.

"Good question."

"I'm not saying that Archie killed anyone," Tara clarified. "In fact, I would be shocked if I found out he had. But if the cat wanted to be sure you had that particular information, I would assume that the fact that Archie was on the island on Tuesday will come into play at some point."

"Maybe Archie saw something." Cassie, who had been shelving some books, joined us. "Maybe the reason the cat wanted you to know that Archie was on the island on Tuesday is because he can provide some information you currently don't have."

"Good point," I admitted. "I'll go into the office and call Finn. He might want to follow up with Archie if he hasn't already."

As it turned out, Finn hadn't spoken to Archie yet, and he wasn't aware that Archie was on the island as early as Tuesday. He told me to thank Watson for the heads-up and said that he would track Archie down that afternoon. He had a few things he wanted to follow up on before he spoke to him, so he would make an appointment to speak to him that afternoon.

After I finished my conversation, I returned to the main sales area, where Willow was chatting with a woman who was accompanied by an adorable child with long red ringlets who appeared to be around three.

"Cait, this is Victoria Wallace," Willow introduced me. "And this little princess is Ariel," she added. "Ariel has her heart set on a kitten, but it seems that the only cats Cassie brought in today are adults. Do you have any kittens available?"

"We will," I answered. I picked up one of our applications. "I have a litter of six kittens who will be altered and ready for adoption in two weeks. If you want to make an appointment to stop by the cat sanctuary, you can take a look at them. If you are interested in adopting one of them, you will need to fill out this application. Kittens are popular and will go fast, so we are allowing prospective parents to reserve one contingent on acceptance of the application."

"Do you have a red kitten?" the little girl asked.

"I don't have a red kitten, but I do have an orange one. She has long hair and a sweet, round face."

"Does she have freckles?" asked the girl who had quite a few freckles of her own.

"I'm not sure. I doubt it, but her hair is so long that even if she had freckles, you wouldn't be able to see them. Her eye color might change, but right now she has bright blue eyes like yours."

The child looked up at her mom. "Can we get her?"

The mother turned to me. "I would like to see the kittens. When can we stop by?"

I looked around the room. "It isn't busy, and we have plenty of help this morning, so we can head over to the sanctuary now if you'd like."

"Please, Mommy?"

The mother nodded. "Okay. I'll follow you."

While it was true that I was on a mission to alter every cat I could get my hands on to try to deal with the island's overpopulation issue, I loved matching up little girls with kittens. I knew in the back of my mind that if the spay and neuter program Aunt Maggie had founded worked as she'd hoped, we'd have fewer kittens to deal with over time, but I'd already decided that as long as there were kittens in our care, I would enjoy and share them.

When I arrived back at the estate, I spotted Cody's car in the drive, so after I showed the woman and her child the kittens and accepted their application, I headed to the cabin to see what my husband was up to.

"You're home." I gave Cody a quick peck on the lips.

"I came by to pick up the kids. I didn't know you'd be here."

"I wasn't planning to be, but there was someone who wanted to look at the kittens. I am planning to go back to the store, but I have time to grab some lunch if you want."

"I have to get back to the newspaper for a conference call about the upcoming island council elections. We can do dinner instead."

I nodded. "That would be nice. I know Danny is working at the bar tonight, and Tara and Cassie are both volunteering at the community haunted house, but we could ask Finn and Siobhan if they want to join us. We could even go to the haunted house."

"Sounds like fun. I really need to run now. Why don't you check with Siobhan and let me know? I'll go ahead and take Max and Watson with me, so they don't have to stay home alone all day. I should be home by five."

I kissed Cody once again as he headed out the door.

Chapter 11

It was busy when I got back to the bookstore, so I pitched in to help. It did seem as if a lot of alumni from all the high school graduating classes were in town for the weekend, and a fair number of them were popping in for coffee after debarking the ferry. It was good to catch up with folks I hadn't seen for years, although it was so crowded that I only had a minute to chat with each customer as they came in. It was late in the day before I remembered that I never had called Siobhan about dinner that evening. I knew that she was working today and was likely to be in her office until four-thirty or five, so I called her cell.

"Cait. I'm glad you called."

"You are? What's up?"

"I've been trying to get hold of Finn, but his cell is going directly to voice mail. I was supposed to pick Connor up at the sitter's at four, but I have two island council members in my office, so I hoped Finn could get him. I don't suppose you can help me out?"

"I'd be happy to." Siobhan's job as mayor was an important one, and if she was asking for her a favor, the council members in her office most likely had something important to discuss.

"Thanks. You're the best. I can either pick him up at the bookstore or at the cabin when I am done here."

"I'll probably just head home. If that changes, I'll text you to let you know."

I hung up with Siobhan and filled Tara in. Cassie was just going out the door, and because she was going home to get ready for the haunted house, she offered to pick up Connor. We were both sure that Siobhan would be home by the time Cassie had to leave, but in the event she wasn't, I told her to call me, and I would come right home. I assumed that Finn was meeting with Owen and Archie. Hadn't he said he planned to track them down this afternoon? I doubted that either was a serious suspect in his mind, so I would think the interviews would be relatively short.

The last ferry of the day pulled in just after Cassie left, so Willow, Tara, and I all pitched in to serve the customers. Willow had to get home to her baby and Tara had to head over to the haunted house, where she'd volunteered for an uncostumed job, so I offered to clean up after checking with Cassie to confirm that Siobhan had gotten home. It was going on six by the time I cleaned the coffee bar and got the cats packed up, so I called Cody to let him know I was on my way. He was already at the cabin, so I asked him if Finn was home yet. I never had gotten around to asking Siobhan about dinner, but if Finn was going to be too late, it wasn't going to work out anyway. Cody informed me that Siobhan had come by with Connor and Finn wasn't home yet, nor could she reach him, and she was getting worried. His office was just around the corner, and I offered to drive by to see if he was there. He wasn't, so I called Cody back to let him know that the office was dark and locked up tight. I wasn't overly worried about Finn; he was a capable guy, but it wasn't like him to be completely unreachable for a long period of time because he knew that Siobhan would be worried about him. Finn had planned to meet with Liza this afternoon, followed by Owen and then Archie, if he was able to set up an appointment. I didn't know how to reach either Liza or Archie, but I could reach Owen, so I offered to call him. I seemed to remember him saying that he was having dinner on Chase's boat this evening, so there was a chance I wouldn't be able to reach him on his cell, but I tried. Surprisingly, he answered almost immediately.

"Owen, it's Caitlin Hart. I'm looking for Finn, and I know he was going to stop by to see you today. Did he ever make it over?"

"He did. I guess he was here at around four. We chatted for a bit, and he must have left here around four thirty. He was going to stop by to see Archie after me, but I am sitting in front of the house Archie is renting and neither he nor Finn seem to be here."

"Was Archie still planning on going with you to the dinner party on Chase's boat?" I asked.

"He was. We were supposed to meet at the marina at five thirty. The shuttle was going to pick us up to take us out to the boat at around that time. When Archie never showed and wasn't answering his phone, I decided to drive out to the house he is renting on the north shore. The place is deserted."

"Do you have any idea where Archie might have gone?"

"Not a clue. And there's more. I peeked inside the house through the window. It is getting dark, and there are no lights on inside, but I could see definite signs of a struggle."

My heart sank. "What is the address where you are now?"

Owen provided it.

"Okay. I'm going to meet you. If either Finn or Archie shows up before I get there, call me."

"Okay. I guess I'll call Becky and let her know we aren't going to make it for dinner as planned."

I called Cody and told him what I knew and was going to do. I warned him not to freak out Siobhan until we knew more. He agreed to be honest but supportive with her. He planned to meet me at the address Owen had provided. I then called Danny and let him know what was going on. The bar was close by, so I arranged to pick him up out front when he offered to make the trip with me.

"So what are we thinking?" Danny asked as soon as he got into the vehicle.

"I don't know. Owen said that Finn was on his way to see Archie, and now neither of them are answering their cells. Owen also said there are signs of a struggle in the house. I don't know what is going on, but I have a feeling it can't be anything good. Cody is meeting us at the house Archie is renting; it didn't make sense for him to come all the way into town to make the trip north with us. I guess we'll assess the situation then and figure out what to do."

By the time Danny and I arrived at the house on the north shore, it was totally dark and Cody was already there. Both he and Owen looked worried. Cody had a flashlight, which he used to peek into the windows. When I got a peek at the interior of the house, I was even more worried than before.

"Should we call someone?" Owen asked. "The sheriff?"

"Maybe," I said. "If we can't find Finn and Archie. I suppose we should look around first. Finn's patrol car isn't here, so if they left together, Finn was driving, and if that's true, there is a good likelihood that he has everything under control."

"Just because Finn's car is gone doesn't mean Finn was driving," Cody pointed out. "Anyone could have been."

I supposed that was true. "Finn's car is equipped with a LoJack. We should be able to find him that way. We can call the sheriff and have someone from the main office do a search, or we can use the computer in Finn's office. It has the software on it."

"Once we call the sheriff, we won't be able to close that can of worms, but it is forty minutes back to Finn's office," Cody said. "A lot can happen in forty minutes."

"I think Siobhan has a key," I said. "I don't want to make things worse, but she is already worried. I'll call her and have her head over to Finn's office. She can bring Connor with her."

"In the meantime, I'm going to look for a way inside," Danny informed us.

"I'll come with you," Owen offered.

It didn't take Siobhan long to make it from the peninsula to Finn's office in Pelican Bay. She'd called our mom and asked her if she would meet her there and then take Connor home with her. Siobhan called me back as soon as she was able to get into Finn's office computer. "The car is at the marina."

"The marina in Harthaven?" I asked.

"No. The small, private one on the north shore."

"Okay, we'll head over there now."

"Mom has Connor, so I'm heading out to meet you. If you end up going somewhere other than the marina, call me."

"I will," I assured her. "And try not to worry. I'm sure Finn is fine." I glanced at Cody. "Siobhan said Finn's car is at the marina on the north shore. If he isn't there, I think we need to call the sheriff."

"Agreed. I'll let the others know what we're doing."

Danny had managed to break into the house through the back door. He'd turned on the lights, and we all looked around briefly. While there were items on the floor that shouldn't have been, indicating a struggle, we didn't find a single drop of blood. Nor did we find anything that would constitute a clue as to what had happened to the men. It was only about five miles from where we were to the marina where Siobhan said we would find Finn's car, so we piled into the vehicles we had and headed in that direction. When we arrived, we found Finn's car in the parking lot. There was no one inside. We used the flashlights Cody and Danny had with them to look around but didn't notice anyone anywhere.

"They probably left in a boat," Danny said.

"They?" Owen said with panic in his voice. "They who? What happened to Archie? Are you saying he has been kidnapped?"

Actually, my thought was that Archie had kidnapped Finn, but I supposed it was possible that some third party had kidnapped them both. Archie did have a job that made him a lot of money, and he was privy to government secrets. It made sense that he was the sort of person that others would think was worth kidnapping. I wasn't sure how Finn would work into a scenario in which a third party was the kidnapper unless he happened to stop by when the kidnapper was at Archie's, and that person was forced to take both men. Archie had value, but Finn, not so much. I hated to think about what a kidnapper might do to him.

I finally answered Owen. "I'm not sure what happened. I think it is important to keep our heads and figure this out. Do you know if Archie has a boat?"

"Not that he ever mentioned."

"Does he have a friend with a boat?"

Owen shrugged. "Maybe. Archie never mentioned that he had one, or access to one when we spoke, but I suppose he might have rented one and not told me about it."

"You said that he arrived on the island on Wednesday."

Owen nodded. "Yes, that's right. But we didn't have plans together until this evening."

"I spoke to a woman this morning who saw him on the island on Tuesday. He was driving a lime-green Lamborghini."

Owen frowned. "Archie does have a green Lamborghini, but he specifically told me he would be arriving on Wednesday. Why would he lie?"

"I don't know. I didn't see the car at the house. Do you know where it might be?"

Owen slowly shook his head. "I have no idea. Are you sure the woman you spoke to wasn't mistaken about Archie being on the island on Tuesday?"

"Honestly, I have no way of knowing for certain what she saw or when she saw it. I have no reason to believe that she would lie. Why would she? But I suppose she could have gotten her dates mixed up. I guess that at this point, the important thing is to find him and Finn. We can sort the rest out from there."

The next hour was intense. Siobhan showed up and was remarkably calm, considering the circumstances. Owen insisted on calling the sheriff, who sent over two men who didn't seem to have any more of a clue about what to do than we did. None of us had recognized either of them, and they looked about as green as a deputy could be, so we had to assume they were new hires doing their time working the islands until they could obtain the experience necessary to apply for a job in one of the larger towns or cities located closer to Seattle. They took a cursory look at Finn's car before warning us to stay out of their way. They told us they were heading to the house Archie had rented and suggested that we might want to go home and let them do the investigating. Owen decided to head back to the rental house and watch from afar, while Cody, Danny, Siobhan, and I stayed at the marina and tried to come up with our own plan.

"Okay, so, what now?" I asked.

"Flip Davidson docks his boat in this marina," Danny said. "It isn't here at the moment, and I would assume he would be in by now if he'd gone fishing, but I can call him on his cell. If he doesn't know anything, I'll call Denver Postman. If Archie leased a short-term slip for the time of his stay, he most likely leased it from Denver."

"I thought the slips were all privately owned by homeowners in the area," I said.

"They are," Danny answered. "But a lot of the homeowners don't actually live on the island, so for a small fee, Denver takes care of keeping the slips leased."

Danny walked away to call Flip and then Denver. I wanted to do something to help, but I really didn't know what. One of the deputies had called the coast guard, although I wasn't sure how much good that would do; we didn't have a description of the boat if there even was one.

"If Archie did kidnap Finn at the rental house and brought him to the marina and loaded him onto a boat, Finn would have had time to leave us a clue of some sort," I said to Siobhan, who had been calling Finn's cell over and over again.

"I agree. Unless he was unconscious."

"I don't think Finn was injured," Cody said.

I wasn't sure if he actually believed that or was just trying to offer Siobhan a theory that would bring her some comfort from the stress she had to be feeling.

"I have to assume he was restrained," Cody continued, "but I didn't notice any blood inside the rental house or in the interior of Finn's car."

"So if Archie was the one who kidnapped Finn, which we don't actually know at this point, then perhaps Finn was surprised by the presence of a gun and was forced to surrender his own weapon and accompany Archie to the boat," Siobhan speculated.

"Exactly," I said. "And if that is the case, it seems like Finn would have tried to leave a clue or a way to figure out what had happened. Has anyone tried to track Finn's phone?"

"I asked one of the deputies if they had done it when I spoke to them about the car," Cody offered. "It appears that his phone is turned off."

"Archie is a smart guy," Siobhan said. "It seems like a dumb move to leave Finn's cruiser at the marina if he did plan an escape from there by boat."

"Siobhan has a good point," I said. "What if the car was left here to intentionally throw us off? What if Finn and Archie are still on the island, but Archie wanted to be sure we'd be looking for him at sea?"

"I suppose that could be what is going on," Cody said.

I watched Danny as he hung up with whoever he'd been talking to and headed back in our direction.

"Any luck?" I asked.

Danny nodded. "I was able to get hold of Flip on his cell. His boat is dry-docked for repair, and he hasn't been to the marina in over two weeks. I called Denver too, and he said there are five slips not currently being leased. He did point out that it is possible that someone could have used one of the slips without going through the proper channels. It isn't like the marina is monitored in the off-season."

"So, what now?" Siobhan asked. "Where do we even start to look?"

I glanced at Cody and Danny, but neither answered.

"Finn's phone has been turned off, and his car is here in the marina," I started. "We suspect he was on the north shore to meet with Archie, although we have not definitively confirmed that Finn was ever at Archie's place. We found signs of a struggle at the house, so we suspect that either Archie kidnapped Finn or a third party kidnapped them both. The lack of a blood trail seems to indicate that no one had been injured yet, although I suppose there are ways to cause injury and even death without spilling any blood."

I glanced at Siobhan, who was beginning to look panicked. I was surprised she had kept it together as long as she had.

"We weren't able to pick up a signal from Finn's phone, but what about Archie's?" Cody asked.

"Owen would have his number, but we'll need someone with the expertise to track the phone," I pointed out.

"I bet someone at the sheriff's office could put a trace on it," Siobhan said.

"Let's call Owen," I suggested. "It seems to me that he wants to find Archie almost as much as we want to find Finn."

Owen not only knew Archie's number but told us that we should ask Becky for help tracking it. He offered to call her to see if she had the equipment she would need to do it on the yacht. It turned out that she did and promised to call him back within a half hour. In the meantime, Cody and Danny took another look around the marina, and I went with Siobhan to her car, where she called our mom to check in.

"Finn is going to be fine," I said to my older sister after she hung up the phone.

"I know. I'm not even freaking out. Not really. Yes, I wish this wasn't happening, but my intuition is telling me that Finn has things under control even if his being in control isn't apparent to us right now." Siobhan slipped her phone into her sweater pocket after checking her messages. I sat in the passenger seat of her car beside her in the driver's seat. "I've been thinking about your comment about Finn leaving us a clue. If his phone is off, he wouldn't have been able to leave us a message of any sort, which, in my mind, is the obvious move for him to have made, but I do agree he would have tried to do something even if his hands were tied."

"If he had been restrained and he had been in the car when it was driven to the marina, he would most likely have been in the back seat. We didn't really search the car. Perhaps we should."

"I agree," Siobhan said. "Let's let Danny and Cody know what we are thinking."

We left Siobhan's car, then headed to the dock, where Cody and Danny were standing around, talking.

"Did you find anything?" I asked.

Danny nodded. "Owen called back. Becky told him that the phone associated with the phone number they both have for Archie is currently on Vancouver Island. She tried calling the phone, but no one answered. She is going to pull the phone records to see if she can pick up a clue that way."

"Vancouver Island is close by boat," I pointed out. "It makes a lot of sense that if someone did kidnap Finn, they might head to Canada."

"So what do we do?" Siobhan asked.

"Owen said the borrowed deputies are waiting for the sheriff to call them back," Danny said. "The sheriff's department doesn't have jurisdiction in Canada, but the sheriff is going to see if he can get local law enforcement on Vancouver Island to check things out."

Chapter 12

Siobhan and I shared our intention of thoroughly searching Finn's car for clues with the guys. Cody and I climbed into the back seat, he with his flashlight and me with the light on my phone. Danny and Siobhan took the front seat. Siobhan turned on the overhead light. We couldn't be sure where Finn had been sitting during the trip from the rental house to the marina. He could have been tied up and put in the back seat, but he could also have been told to drive while the person who kidnapped him held a gun on him.

I wasn't sure what we were looking for. Anything that stood out as unusual, I supposed. I imagined that Finn wouldn't have had a lot of time or freedom to leave a really good clue, so if he did leave something behind, it would be subtle.

"This may be a waste of time," Danny said. "Chances are that if Archie is on Vancouver Island, Finn is as well."

"Maybe, but we don't even know for sure that Archie is on the island," I pointed out. "The car being left in the marina paired with the GPS for Archie's phone showing up on Vancouver Island does seem to suggest that Archie and Finn and perhaps a third party left Madrona Island by boat and headed to Canada, but that also seems a bit too convenient, not to mention sloppy."

"Cait is right," Siobhan said. "Archie is some sort of genius who works for the government. It seems to me that if he lives a covert life, he would be more careful with the clues he left behind."

"Unless the clues are decoys," Cody added.

"Exactly," I said, as I shoved my hand under the seat and felt around on the carpet. Cody was shining his flashlight into the little cubbyholes on the door near the cup holder.

"I found something," I said, wrapping my hand around the object and pulling it toward me. "A quarter. I don't suppose this is a clue."

"Probably not," Cody said. "I found a straw in the door panel, but like the quarter, I suspect it was just left behind during the normal course of a day."

"Of course, the car is a sheriff's department cruiser," Danny pointed out. "I doubt Finn allows the sort of people who ride in the back seat to use straws."

"He might," Siobhan countered. "I know the back seat is supposed to be reserved for people who have been arrested or taken in for questioning, but Finn gives rides to others sometimes as well."

Danny slid his hand into the opening between the seat and the seat back on the passenger side of the front. The car was cleaned regularly, so anything we found would be a few days' old at the most.

"I found something." Siobhan slid down onto the floor from the front driver's seat. When she reappeared, she was holding a tie clip.

"Is that Finn's?" I asked.

Siobhan put her hand to her mouth. She nodded as tears gathered in the corners of her eyes. "I gave it to him for our one-year wedding anniversary. I told him it was my way of reminding him that I was at home waiting for him no matter how late his responsibility to the island might keep him out." Siobhan let out a tiny laugh. "Of course, he pointed out that it was probably my responsibilities as mayor that would keep me out late rather than the other way around, but he has worn this tie clip every day since I gave it to him." She ran her fingers over it. "Well, at least every day that he has worn a tie, which is pretty much just workdays and weddings."

"Okay, so it could very well be that he worked the clip free and left it behind," I said. "I suppose it could have simply fallen off if there was a struggle, but I'm going to choose to think it is an intentional clue."

"Yes, but a clue that is telling us what?" Danny asked.

Siobhan stared at the tie clip as if willing it to speak to us. Naturally, it didn't. But I think she knew, as I did, that Finn wouldn't have bothered to have left the clip behind unless it was able to serve as a message.

"I guess if Finn intentionally left the tie clip behind and it was found on the floor of the driver's side of the vehicle, that tells us that Finn had his hands free and that he most likely drove to this location," Cody pointed out.

"The car is pointed away from the water," I said. "I suppose that the person who would have had a gun on Finn could have directed him to park as he did, but it is equally likely that Finn parked in the opposite direction of the marked parking lines for a reason."

"The car is not only parked across the marked parking lines, but it is facing east," Danny mused. "The entrance is to the west. It does seem as if the direction in which the car is parked could be a clue if, in fact, we can assume from the tie clip being left on the driver's side floor that Finn was the one who was driving."

"Okay, so if the point of all this is that Finn wanted us to know he was the one who drove to the marina, how can that information help us find him now?" Siobhan asked.

"If Finn was the one driving, which means his hands were free, he had access to all the equipment in the dashboard, not just the ignition and steering wheel," I pointed out. "Sure, the kidnapper must have been watching him, but it still might have been possible for Finn to flip a switch or turn a knob while going about the normal operations of the vehicle."

Siobhan sat straight in the driver's seat. She put her hands on the wheel and then sat perfectly still. Her eyes narrowed in on the air vent for the air conditioning. She shone the light from the cellphone toward the vent. "I think there is something in here. It looks like a gum wrapper."

Finn did carry gum on him at all times. In fact, at any given moment, unless he was at home in his own house, you could be sure to find a pack of gum in his pocket. "Can you get it?" Danny asked.

"I can try, but I can't get a finger inside."

"I have my keys," Danny offered. "If I'm careful, I can probably wedge it out with a key. It is just as likely I'll end up shoving it farther into the vent, though, but unless someone has something better, a key seems to be our best bet."

Something like needle-nose pliers would have been best, but we didn't have any tools. Danny and Siobhan changed places, and Danny began to work his key into the plastic slats covering the vent. It took several minutes and more than one start, but finally, Danny was able to work the gum wrapper free. It was folded, so he opened it and looked at it. "The letters MAP are scratched into the silver part on the outside of the wrapper."

"Map?" I asked. "What could he mean by a map? Does he want us to consult a map, and if so, which map? Was there a map in the house where Archie was staying?"

"The map in the car," Siobhan said. "The car has a GPS system that tracks not only where the car is at that moment but where it *has been*. I need to call the sheriff's office again."

Siobhan did that while the rest of us waited. After a bit of back and forth with the night dispatcher, she eventually was able to get through to the right person. Luckily, the county deputy on shift that night was someone Siobhan knew who was willing to give her the information she was looking for without making her jump through a bunch of hoops. Even with his cooperation, it took almost thirty minutes to find out that Finn's car had traveled from Owen's photography studio to the house Archie had been renting, to the marina where it still sat.

"That makes no sense," Danny said. "Why would Finn tell us to look at the map if he didn't go anywhere we wouldn't have already known about?"

"Maybe Finn was referring to something other than the car's mapping system," Cody suggested.

"There would be a map on his phone, but we already know it is turned off," I said. "There aren't any other maps in the car. At least none that we've found, and we've gone through things pretty thoroughly. There could be a map back at the house he wants us to find. We could head back and look around there. Maybe the kidnapper was using a map, and Finn remembered that he'd left it open on the desk, or maybe on one of the countertops. Somewhere visible that might provide us with a clue to where they would be heading."

"The borrowed deputies are at the house," Danny pointed out. "If there was something to find, they probably already messed with it. Besides, I had the feeling they didn't want us hanging around. They probably assumed that we'd leave here and head back to the south shore or they'd be here telling us not to touch anything."

"I guess we could call Owen again," Siobhan suggested. "He was at the house the last time we spoke to him. He might still be there, and if he is, he might be able to give us an idea of what is happening there."

"What if he is in on this somehow?" I asked.

"In on it, how?" Cody asked.

I shrugged. "I don't know. If Archie did kidnap Finn, maybe Owen is helping him. They have been friends for a long time."

"Owen is the one who let us know that Archie was missing in the first place," Danny reminded me. "Why would he do that if he wanted to help Archie disappear?"

"I guess he wouldn't," I had to admit.

"Whether Owen was in on whatever is going on or not, the important thing now is to find Finn," Siobhan reminded us. "If he is directing us toward some map, we need to figure out a way to gain access to it."

"Okay," I said. "Let's head back to the house and see what we can find."

As could have been predicted, when we arrived at the house Archie had been renting, the borrowed deputies refused to allow us inside. Owen was sitting alone in his own car, and he told us that he was just getting ready to leave. Becky was going to send a shuttle for him to the marina in Harthaven so he could be with his friends while they waited for Archie to be found. In a way, the fact that he was going to walk away from the investigation seemed odd, but not everyone wanted to roll up their sleeves and get their hands dirty the way the Scooby gang did.

"So if we can't get into the house to look for a map, what do we do now?" I asked after Owen drove off.

No one spoke, I imagined because no one had any ideas.

"Can I see the gum wrapper again?" I held out my hand to Siobhan.

She handed it to me. I unfolded it and took a look at it. "The word MAP is in all caps," I pointed out. "I wonder if we are reading this right. Maybe the idea isn't to find a map but somewhere represented by the acronym MAP."

"Like where?" Danny asked.

"Madrona Athletic Park," I suggested. "I don't know why Finn would want us to go there; that is just one example."

"Madrona Allied Power," Cody added. "I suppose that whatever is going on could have to do with our floundering power company. You know they are on the verge of bankruptcy."

I didn't know that and wondered what it would mean for the island if the local power company did go under. I supposed the area's residents would need to hook up to the county power source, which would be expensive, but that was a subject to worry about on another day.

"What about the airport?" Siobhan said.

"Yes, the airport," I agreed. "The code for our little municipal airport is MAP."

"That has to be it," Cody joined in.

"It's ingenious really," Danny said. "If Archie is behind the kidnapping and he is planning to fly off the island, which we all know he has the resources to do, leaving Finn's car at the marina is the perfect decoy."

"Let's go," Danny suggested.

"I'll ride with Siobhan," I offered, so my sister wouldn't need to make the drive back down to Harthaven on her own.

Chapter 13

When Siobhan, Danny, Cody, and I arrived at the small airport, we found Finn in one of the hangers. He'd been tied up and gagged and was mad as heck, but at least he didn't appear to be hurt.

"Finn," Siobhan yelled before running over to where he was sitting on a chair. She pulled the gag from his mouth.

"You found my message in the AC vent," he said as he rubbed his wrists where the rope that had secured him had left burn marks.

"We did," Siobhan said, crying in relief while Cody untied his ankles.

"Where is Archie?" Danny asked once Finn was able to stand up.

"Long gone. As it turns out, Archie is the one who killed Winifred Westminster."

"Archie killed Amy?" I asked, totally shocked by the revelation. I guess I'd considered the possibility after we'd found both Finn and Archie missing, but from my immediate feelings of disbelief, I hadn't really believed it.

Finn shook his head. "Not Amy, just Winifred."

"Archie killed Winifred, but he didn't kill Amy?" Cody clarified.

Finn nodded. "Archie admitted to killing Ms. Westminster but denied killing Amy."

"But why would Archie kill Winnie?" I wondered.

Finn walked toward the large door at one end of the hanger. He looked out at the landscape as if to ensure himself that Archie really was gone, and then answered. "It seems that while investigating Amy's death, Winifred did some digging into each of the suspects on her list. Apparently, she found something sensitive about Archie that he did not want to be made public."

"What?" Siobhan asked.

"He wouldn't say what it was, but I plan to do my own digging to find out. What I do know is that Archie panicked when he found out that Winifred had not only stumbled across something she shouldn't have but planned to cash in on it."

"Cash in on it?" I asked.

"She planned to make it public in her book. From what I overheard Archie telling someone on the phone, he went to her place and tried to convince her to keep what she knew to herself and, when she refused, he killed her."

"He killed her and then what?" Danny asked.

"And then he planned to take off. He had a jet on the way to pick him up when I showed up to talk to him. I'm not really sure why I picked up on his odd behavior, but I did. I guess I started asking questions he wasn't prepared to answer. At some point, I realized he had a gun, which caught me off guard. He quickly got the upper hand, taking my gun."

"At least he didn't shoot you," Siobhan said.

"He made it clear from the very beginning that he meant me no harm. I guess he realized he would need a decoy, so he made me drive to the marina, where we were met by a man named Jovan. I overheard them talking and realized that we weren't leaving in a boat as I'd originally thought, but the plan was to leave my car at the marina as a decoy while Jovan took us to the airport. I had about thirty seconds with no one watching me, so I scratched the note on the gum wrapper in my pocket. I slipped it into the AC vent just in case they decided to check the floor where I had been sitting. Once I had done that, I dropped my tie clip, hoping that someone would see it and take a closer look."

"What if the men did search the floor and found the tie clip?" I asked.

"I figured that if they found it, I could just say it had fallen off. If they had found the gum wrapper with the word MAP on it, they would figure out what I was trying to do. As it turned out, they didn't search the area where I had been sitting at all, so I could have just left a note on the floor. I think they were confident about getting away."

"So Archie flew to Canada?" Danny asked.

"I don't think he went to Canada," Finn said. "As I said, I'm pretty sure that everything that you think you know about where he went is just an illusion."

"But his phone was tracked to Canada. Vancouver Island to be exact," I informed Finn.

"I'm sure he probably just made it appear that way. He might have used some sort of high-level cloning, or maybe he was able to hack into the GPS system. Archie is a brilliant man. He knows all the tricks of the trade. He has friends in high places. He wanted everyone looking for him in Canada. I don't know for certain where he is now, but I do know he is not going to be easy to track down."

Siobhan frowned. "You aren't going to try to track him down yourself?"

"No. I'll leave that to the government. To be honest, based on what I overheard, I think it may be possible that someone from the government actually helped Archie to get off the island. If not, if Archie acted alone, I suspect the folks from the NSA aren't going to be happy to find that one of their highest-ranking assets is in the wind."

"Did Archie ever say exactly what he did for the NSA?" Danny asked.

Finn shook his head. "He was intentionally vague. I'm sort of surprised he told me what he did. He could have just shot me and been done with it, but it seemed like he wanted me to know that he didn't want to kill Winifred, but she forced his hand. I had the impression he felt remorse for the way things worked out. I don't know what Ms. Westminster found out about Archie, but I suspect that in the end, it will be determined that Archie was right to protect his secret."

Okay, now I really wanted to know what Winnie had discovered. I wondered if she'd left notes somewhere and if she had, whether a nosy, industrious person such as myself might be able to find them.

Chapter 14

Saturday, October 26

Saturday dawned drizzly and overcast. The homecoming game was scheduled for four o'clock in the afternoon, so I hoped the weather cleared by then. On any other morning I might have enjoyed lingering with Cody, Max, and Watson, but today I had a lot to do if I was going to figure out who had killed Amy and make it to the game on time, so I rolled myself out of bed despite the fact that it was still dark and my cabinmates were all still sleeping. I was not delusional and did realize that it would be close to impossible to solve a fifteen-year-old murder in just one day, but I was motivated to try.

Tara and I had decided to open the bookstore early. We normally closed at five on Saturdays, but we had decided to close early today, at two o'clock, which would give us time to go home and change before heading to the game. With all the pomp and circumstance added to the pregame and halftime festivities, the gang wouldn't gather at the bar for the after-party until around eight. Danny, Aiden, Tara, and I had discussed it and decided to offer pizza and chicken wing appetizers in addition to the libations the boys had picked out to showcase.

Poor Max was going to be stuck in the house alone for much of the day, so despite the drizzle, I bundled up and took him out for a walk. Cody planned to spend some time at the newspaper office this morning, so I left him a note, asking him to text me later if we missed each other. Although it was cool and wet this morning, Max and I thoroughly enjoyed our time by the sea. There is nothing quite like welcoming the day as the sun pokes its head over the horizon.

Of course, today there was no sun, but somehow I didn't mind. As Max and I passed Mr. Parsons's house, I wondered how he was doing. When Cody and I had told him about our plans to remodel and the fact that we wanted him to stay with our friend, Balthazar Pottage, during the construction, he hadn't batted an eye. If he had refused our request that he move out temporarily, I wouldn't have blamed him at all—it was, after all, his home—but Mr. Parsons had mellowed since Cody had moved in, and except for a moment here and there, something we all have, he'd become about as pleasant and agreeable as anyone I knew.

I hurried my step a bit to catch up with Max, who had gone off to chase some geese. Mr. Parsons wanted the construction to be complete before Christmas so we could host our annual holiday meal. The first two years, the dinner had been on Christmas

Eve, but last year we'd been in Florida for Christmas, so we'd moved it to Thanksgiving. It had been nice, but I think everyone hoped the feast would move back to Christmas Eve this year.

Once Max arrived at the rocky area that divided the peninsula from the southern part of the island, I turned around and headed back. Thinking about Mr. Parsons's annual party made me think of the holiday season in general. The children's church choir Cody and I organized had the script of a holiday play to learn, as well as the new songs we planned to debut at the Christmas service. I supposed we'd need to hit the ground running once we got through the next week of homecoming and Halloween.

As I approached the cabin, I thought about the day ahead. I wondered where I would even start to dig into the complexity of Amy Anderson's murder. There was a part of me that just wanted to forget the investigation and enjoy the rest of the weekend, but there was another part that wanted justice for the young girl who had died before she'd even gotten started.

I took off my sandy shoes and entered the cabin in my stocking feet. I could hear Cody in the shower, so I made a pot of coffee, fed Max and Watson, and then took out my phone to check for messages. There was one from Cassie, letting me know that she'd taken care of the cats in the sanctuary while Max and I were walking, and another from Finn, saying that he'd turned the Archie Baldwin case over to the FBI and planned to let them figure it out. It was sort of anticlimactic when you invested time and effort in an investigation and then were forced to walk away before it was over, but I had the idea that whatever was going on with Archie was above my pay grade, so I vowed to let it go.

Watson crawled into my lap and began to purr once I'd settled in near the window with my coffee. The cats who were sent to help me solve mysteries all seemed to have their own personalities. Some were cuddly and wanted as much affection as they could get, while others tended to be standoffish. Some were helpful and wanted to be involved in the murder investigation to the point of being pushy, while others watched from the sidelines until it was time to provide that one clue that would change everything. So far, it seemed as if Watson was somewhere in the middle.

As I sipped my coffee and watched the drizzle turn into a steady rain outside, I considered the suspects I felt should still be considering in the Amy Anderson case. Strangely, in my mind the fact that Archie had killed Winifred Westminster for a reason totally unconnected to Amy made him seem innocent in her murder. I also felt that we needed to remove Becky from the suspect list. She had helped us last night, as had Owen. Not that any of them really was on the list to begin with, but my need to introduce organization into my life seemed to demand I formally clear them.

I went over all the names in my mind. Lance Larson had the opportunity, probably more than anyone else. And then there was Liza Tisdale. She seemed to have a motive at the time, and Finn had had an appointment to speak to her yesterday, but I never got around to asking him how that interview had gone. I supposed I'd need to make time to ask him today. There were those such as Brock Stevenson who we'd crossed off the list because they hadn't been on the island to kill Winnie, but now that we knew that Amy and Winnie were killed by different people, should we put him and the others back on the list?

To me, the best suspects were Coach Brown and Dirk Gleason. I wasn't sure why I suspected them above the others; it just seemed odd they were at the party in the first place.

Maybe Finn would make some progress figuring out who had killed Amy before the kickoff of the big game. I certainly hoped that would be the case. If the killer was someone who was not currently living on the island, chances were they would leave after the game was over. Of course, now that we knew that Winnie and Amy were killed by different people, that really opened up the field of suspects. Initially, we'd only listed individuals who had been at the party and on the island when Winnie died. When I really stopped to think about the fact that the person who'd killed Amy could have been anyone at the party, it hit me how completely impossible it was going to be to find the killer after all these years.

I put my hands around Watson's thin frame and lifted him up, so we were eye to eye. "Okay, buddy, it's fourth and ten with only minutes remaining in the game. It seems to me if we are going to pull off a victory here, it is really up to you. When I thought that the same person had killed both Amy and Winnie, figuring out who the guilty party seemed doable. Now... well, now figuring out who killed Amy seems impossible."

"Meow."

I set Watson on the floor. I knew that when working with Tansy's magical cats, the timing couldn't be forced, but I still hoped he'd give me something to noodle on before I left for the bookstore.

"It must be raining," Cody said as he walked into the main living area of the cabin from the bathroom, kissing me gently on the lips and running a hand over my damp, limp hair.

"It was drizzling during our walk, but I'm hoping it will clear up by game time. Are you still planning to go in to the newspaper?"

"I am. I hope to be done with my work by around noon. Are you still going in to the bookstore?"

I nodded. "After I shower." I glanced at Watson. "Unless, of course, I can figure out how to activate our detective kitty here, in which case I figure I'll let Tara handle the bookstore while I solve Amy's murder."

Cody poured coffee into a travel mug. "If you do pick up a new clue, call me. I don't want you going off sleuthing by yourself."

"I will," I promised. I picked up the list I had made after our last brainstorming session. "Now that we know that Amy and Winnie were killed by different people, do you think we should modify the list to include people who could have killed Amy but weren't on the island to kill Winnie? People like Brock?"

Cody frowned. "I will admit that now that we know Amy and Winnie weren't killed by the same person, it really opens up the suspect pool. Maybe too much. Tripp wasn't able to solve Amy's murder fifteen years ago, and no one has been able to solve it since. Maybe it isn't doable."

"All murders are solvable if you have the right information." I glanced at Watson. "I think I'll take Watson into town with me when I go. He might be more apt to point me in the right direction if he has more to work with. I don't suppose you want to take Max with you?"

Cody nodded. "Yeah, I'll take him. Just remember, if you do decide to go sleuthing rather than heading to the bookstore, call me."

After Cody left, I jumped into the shower. I thought about the fact that Finn had said Tripp had thought Coach Brown was a strong suspect at the time of Amy's murder. I wondered if Tripp had other strong suspects that we didn't know about. Perhaps it would be worth my while to have a conversation with him. Tripp spent most days fishing, but with today's gloomy weather, I sort of doubted he'd be out, so I texted him to ask if I could buy him breakfast. He texted back and said that he loved the idea, so I arranged to meet him at the Driftwood Café. I then called Tara to let her know that I might be late coming in but would drop Watson and the two cats I planned to feature in the lounge by the bookstore on my way to my breakfast meeting with our retired island deputy.

Chapter 15

Tripp Brimmer had been the resident deputy for Madrona Island for a lot of years before he retired. He was a lot rougher around the edges than Finn, and I was aware that during his time as the resident deputy he had sometimes blurred the line when it came to a decision to do the legal thing or the right thing. Truth be told, there were times when Tripp had ignored the line completely.

Once he'd retired and Finn had taken over in his job, Tripp began spending his days playing poker and fishing, but he still kept his ear to the ground and more often than not, he knew exactly who was doing what on the island.

"Thanks for meeting me," I greeted him as I slid into the booth across from him.

"Thanks for inviting me to breakfast." Tripp took a sip of his coffee. "I assume you have asked me here to discuss the Amy Anderson murder case."

I nodded. "I guess you know about Winifred Westminster."

"I do. I have to say I'm surprised. Or at least I was at first. When Archie lived on the island, I thought of him as weak, but from what I can tell, he has grown up and has quite the reputation for being one of those indispensable individuals whose roles are too delicate to make public."

"I heard he worked for the NSA. I don't suppose you know precisely what he does?"

"I'm afraid I really don't, but I did suspect that if Archie shot Winifred Westminster, he had a good reason to do it, and Finn will be getting a call from someone higher up the food chain telling him to close the murder case."

I furrowed my brow. "So you think Archie is going to get away with killing Winnie?"

"I think if she dug up sensitive information and threatened to go public with it, Archie had to deal with her, then yes, I think the whole thing will be swept under the rug."

"That doesn't seem right. I feel like Archie could have handled things differently. If Winnie had information she shouldn't have had, it seems like she could have been detained or debriefed or something."

Tripp shrugged. "Perhaps. It's hard to say what should have occurred with the limited amount of information we have. But Archie killing Winifred Westminster is not why you invited me here."

"That's true," I admitted. "Whatever does or does not happen to Archie as a result of Winnie's death is out of my hands. I wanted to talk to you about Amy's death. I know that you investigated the murder when it happened. I know you were never able to make an arrest, but I am curious as to who you considered to be your primary suspects."

"Does Finn know you are digging around in this?"

I bobbed my head ever so slightly. "Yes and no. He knows that the gang and I are looking into Amy's murder. He doesn't know I invited you to breakfast. I know Finn already spoke to you about this, but now that we're aware that Amy's and Winnie's murder are not connected, I feel like the number of suspects has more than doubled. In fact, it has probably more than tripled. I am just looking for a way to narrow things down a bit."

Tripp nodded. "Fair enough. Let's order, and then I'll tell you what I know."

He ordered eggs Benedict, and I ordered oatmeal and toast. As soon as we'd placed our orders, he began to speak. "Initially, I looked at every single person who attended that party for any amount of time, including you and your friends."

"Yes. I remember that you spoke to Tara and me, and I understand why you felt the need to chat with everyone. But I'm more interested in the list you were left with after your initial interviews."

"I had maybe ten or twelve people I wanted to look at further, but in the end, it really came down to three primary suspects and two secondary ones in my mind."

I sat forward just a bit. "And who were those five people and why did you suspect them?"

"My number one suspect was Dalton Brown. As you know, he worked at the high school as a coach and physical education teacher. While the length of his visit at the party was debated, those I spoke to agreed that it was odd that he was at the party at all.

Sure, it was his football team who won the game that led to them winning the state championship, so one could argue that his showing up to congratulate the team could have been expected, but I spoke to quite a few people who saw Coach Brown out in the yard drinking and smoking pot with the guys hours after he first arrived."

"Did you ask him about that?" I wondered.

"I did. He said he stopped by, chatted with his guys for a bit, and then left. I asked if he'd spent time in the backyard of the house after he left the party inside, and he said he did stop by to chat with a few of the guys he'd missed, but he didn't stay long, and he never went back inside after he left the first time, so he couldn't have killed Amy, who, as we know, was found in an upstairs bedroom. I received varying responses about how long Brown actually was at the party, but everyone agreed that once he left the house, he never went back inside, and I had multiple witnesses who said they saw Amy after Coach Brown left."

"He didn't need to go back inside," I pointed out. "He could have climbed the ladder off the master deck."

Tripp raised a brow. "You found out about that, did you? Yes, you are correct; Coach Brown, or someone else, for that matter, could have accessed the master bedroom where Amy's body was found via the fire escape ladder."

"So anyone could have killed her? Possibly even someone who wasn't actually at the party? I know that would be unlikely, but it would have been possible, right?"

Tripp nodded. "It would have been possible. Which is why I focused on motive when faced with the task of figuring out who had killed Amy."

"And Coach Brown had a motive?"

"It seemed he might have. During the course of interviewing the teens who attended the party, I learned that Amy had confided in one of her friends that she had been sleeping with one of the staff members at the high school. Everyone I spoke to suspected it was Coach Brown, who had been observed eyeing her on numerous occasions. Though one of her friends assured me that while Amy *had* been sleeping with a high school staff member, that person wasn't Coach Brown."

"If not Coach Brown then who?" I asked.

"The friend wouldn't say. She indicated that Amy really cared about the guy and wouldn't want him to get into trouble for sleeping with a student so, despite the fact that I tried quite hard to get a name out of her, she refused to provide one."

I assumed the friend Tripp was referring to was Lexi, but he didn't volunteer the information, and I didn't ask. "Okay, so it looks as if the rumor that Amy was sleeping with Coach Brown might not be true, but it does sound as if he might have been interested in her if numerous students were aware of him noticing her. Were you ever able to verify this?"

"No. I spoke to Coach Brown, he denied doing or saying anything to Amy that could be construed as sexual, and I had conflicting reports, so the eyewitness statements never led to anything."

I paused to let this roll around in my mind. "I suppose that Coach Brown might have shown up at the party and realized that not only was Amy there but she was smashed. If he was interested in her, he might have realized that he had a shot with her, given her state of inebriation. I don't know how he could have found out that she was in the master bedroom, but if he did end up with that bit of information, and if he noticed the exterior ladder, he might have decided to scratch an itch by trying to rape her. She might have fought back and, in a moment of panic, Coach Brown might have suffocated her."

"Basically, that is the conclusion I came to when I investigated the murder. The problem was, I couldn't find a single person who would admit to having seen Coach Brown near the ladder or inside the house after he left, and the reports of the time of his leaving the house were so varied as to be useless."

I took a breath and blew it out slowly. "Okay, I can see why you considered Coach Brown to be a strong suspect."

Our conversation paused when breakfast was delivered. As soon as the server left, I asked Tripp about the other individuals he considered to be suspects.

"My number two suspect was Lance Larson. The party took place at his house, and he was the only one with access to the locked bedroom. Lance admitted that he allowed Amy to lay down in there when she started feeling ill, and he was the one to find her body the following morning. Logic would dictate that if he was the one to kill her, he would have moved the body or even buried it rather than calling the police when he woke the next morning and found her there, but there were other kids still passed out around the house. Moving the body might not have been possible, so instead of trying to cover up the murder, he might have gotten out in front of it when he realized that someone was going to come around looking for her at some point."

"That makes sense. What did Lance say when you spoke to him?"

"He denied having anything to do with Amy's death. He said she came to him and told him that she felt dizzy and nauseated. She asked if there was somewhere quiet where she could lay down, and he decided to let her lay down in his parents' room. He used a key to unlock the door, then pulled it closed behind him after he got Amy settled and left. The door locked automatically. Amy would have been able to get out, but no one other than him should have been able to get in. I asked Lance if it was possible that Amy had let someone into the room, and he admitted it was, although he felt that if someone had been let into the room after he left, that person would have been seen by those waiting in line for the bathroom. I also asked him if the door between the bedroom and the deck had been locked, and he said it should have been, but it was possible that Amy had wanted some fresh air and opened it."

"Was the door open the following morning?"

"It was unlocked when I checked it, which was after the emergency crew had shown up and removed the body. According to Lance, he didn't think to check it when he let Amy into the room, and he didn't check it when he entered the room the next day and found the body, so it is hard to say exactly when it was unlocked. It is even possible that his parents left the slider onto the deck unlocked when they left, and Lance wasn't aware of the fact. Keep in mind, they didn't know their son planned to have a party, so they may not have thought to check it."

I took several bites of my oatmeal, which was getting cold by this point. In my mind, if Coach Brown actually had been coming on to Amy, he made an excellent suspect, even though it would have been tricky to access the room via the fire ladder without being seen. We didn't know exactly when Amy died, so he could have left and come back. Lance seemed to be the only one who had easy access to Amy, but I didn't see that he had a motive. I asked Tripp if Lance's motive was ever determined.

"No," Tripp answered. "I never did come across a reason for Lance to have killed Amy, although sometimes people who are drinking and doing drugs don't need a motive. He could simply have gone into the bedroom to see if Amy was still there, found her sleeping, and figured this was his chance to get with one of the most promiscuous girls in the high school. If she rejected him after he had been so nice to her, he might have retaliated with a pillow to the face, or maybe he tried to force her, and she tried to scream, so he stifled her. The theory is thin but possible, given the overall situation."

"Okay." I nibbled on the corner of my toast. "So we have Coach Brown and Lance Larson as suspects. Who else was in the top three?"

"Dirk Gleason. He showed up at the party late, after Amy had already gone upstairs. One of the girls I interviewed told me that he came in, grabbed a drink, and headed upstairs. He didn't come downstairs until he left the party, approximately thirty minutes later. I asked everyone else about Dirk but was unable to find anyone who had seen him during that half hour. When I asked him why he had come to the party and what he was doing while he was upstairs, he told me that he had a private matter to attend to. If he wasn't killing Amy, I suspect he was at the party to sell drugs, but I could never get him to admit to either. When I tried to push the subject, he told me to arrest him or leave him alone. I didn't have enough to arrest him, so I had to drop it."

It did seem odd that he'd shown up at a party to which he hadn't been invited, immediately gone upstairs and disappeared for thirty minutes, and then left without taking time to hang out with anyone. I thought Coach Brown, Lance, and Dirk all made decent suspects.

"And the two suspects you felt were second tier?" I asked.

"Brock Stevenson and Chase Carter. I never could come up with any compelling evidence that either of them was even upstairs that night, but according to witness statements, Brock was in a foul mood from the minute he arrived, and Chase seemed likely to have accepted what Amy was so blatantly offering."

"Brock was Amy's ex, and I do remember that he was pretty mad about the way she was acting. I also remember that Amy was all over Chase. I suppose it makes sense that either of them might have followed Amy upstairs. I really don't see either of them killing her, but as you've already pointed out, there was a lot of alcohol and of drugs of various kinds circulating that evening, so maybe… So, after all these years, knowing what you know now if you had to choose one of these suspects, who would you go with?"

Tripp paused before answering. "If my intel about Coach Brown was correct, and he had a sexual interest in Amy, my money would be on him. If my witnesses were wrong and he was innocent of eyeing the victim, I guess I'd have to go with either Lance or Dirk. The fact that everyone was wasted out of their minds and their memories of what occurred were blurred complicated things. I talked to a lot of people but finally concluded there wasn't a viable suspect to be found."

"I do remember that everyone was drunk, but it still seems like someone has to have seen something. We do have a timeline of sorts. We can probably figure out what time Lance let Amy into the bedroom, and we know she was murdered at around eleven. It just seems that there should be a way to narrow things down enough to at least make an educated guess."

Chapter 16

I headed to the bookstore after I left the diner. The first ferry of the day would be along soon, and I wanted to be there to help with the rush if possible. I didn't feel that I'd learned much that I hadn't already known from speaking to Tripp, but our conversation had caused me to wonder if perhaps I shouldn't have a heart-to-heart with Lexi. I suspected that she was the one to tell Tripp about the teacher who wasn't Coach Brown who Amy had been having an affair with. I wasn't surprised she hadn't revealed more than she had. She was, after all, Amy's best friend and confidante. But a lot of time had passed, so maybe after all these years, I could convince her to confide in me. I had several theories of who the high school staff member Amy had been having a relationship with might have been. Amy tended to get around, so I wasn't surprised she had done what Tripp seemed to believe she had, but I would be surprised to find out that any of the three youngish teachers on staff at that time would have entered into an affair with a student.

"How'd it go?" Tara asked when I arrived at Coffee Cat Books.

I filled her in while I tied my pink Coffee Cat Books apron around my waist. The ferry had just pulled into view, so I knew we only had about fifteen minutes before the masses began filing into the store. "I came away from the meeting with the realization that I need to call Lexi to see if she will talk with me. I don't know for certain that she will be any more willing to share the secrets she was unwilling to reveal fifteen years ago, but maybe…"

"She is probably going to be at the game today," Tara reminded me. "Maybe you can pull her aside."

"There will be too many people around. I think I'll call her after we deal with the folks from the ferry to see if she can see me this morning." I picked up an empty bottle that had at one point held pumpkin-flavored syrup. "Do we have more syrup for the pumpkin lattes?"

"In the back. Cassie is in the storeroom unpacking the supplies that were delivered yesterday. If you are going back for the syrup, let her know the ferry is here."

After doing a quick inventory to see if we were low on any other supplies, I headed toward the back room. "Ferry is just pulling up," I said to my younger sister.

"Okay. Let me just check off the items in this box."

I grabbed the bottle of pumpkin syrup and then began looking for the cinnamon syrup. "Did you notice where Watson got off to?"

"The last time I saw him, he was sleeping on the sofa in the cat lounge. I noticed that he seems to get along well with the other cats. He appears to be a stray now, but I have to believe that at one point he lived in a home with other animals."

"I had the same thought." I grabbed the cinnamon syrup I was looking for. "Grab some more cups. I think we have plenty of small, but we are low on medium and large."

Cassie did as I asked, then followed me out to the front. The next hour was a busy one, as visitors stopped in for a coffee beverage, a book, or a novelty item as they arrived on the island. Once most of the crowd had dissipated, I headed to the cat lounge to check in with both Watson and the two adoptable felines. Since we opened the store and began showcasing our rescues in the cat lounge, the number of cats living long-term at the sanctuary had dwindled to only those that were truly unadoptable.

"Excuse me." An elderly woman sipping an iced coffee stepped up to me. "Is this cat available for adoption?"

"Unfortunately, he is not one of our available cats." It figured that the woman would hone in on Watson. "The other two are available, and I have several cats and two litters of kittens back at the sanctuary if you would like to meet some of the others."

"I'm not really interested in a kitten," the white-haired woman informed me. "I don't get around as well as I used to, so I'd prefer a low-energy cat who is happy curled up on the sofa with me."

I glanced at the two cats that I'd brought in that morning, who were lounging on the sofa. "Both the cats here today are younger ones who like to play, but I have some older cats at the sanctuary if you want to stop by at some point. Do you live on the island?"

"I live on Lopez Island, but I can come over on the ferry on most any day. Perhaps one day next week?"

"I'll give you my cell number. If you want to call me on Monday, we can make an appointment."

The woman gave Watson one last cuddle, took my number, and left. I picked up Watson and snuggled him to my chest. I had to admit that the woman's assessment of Watson as a low-energy cat had been spot-on. He did like to cuddle, and I really hadn't seen him play much since he'd been with me. "The lady who came in seemed nice. I'm sure the two of you would get along just fine. You know if we can catch this killer, we can work on finding you a permanent home. Wouldn't that be nice?"

"Meow."

"I think we need to wrap up this case today if at all possible." I set the cat down on the floor. "Grab some food or use the cat box if you need to because once I get back, we are going to come up with a game plan."

I called Lexi, but as it turned out, she wasn't home. I called her cell, but she didn't answer that either, so I left a message on her voice mail and went back into the main room, where Tara and Cassie were chatting about the party at the bar that evening. Watson curled back up on the sofa and went to sleep, so I stopped to let them know that I hoped I could find a way to ignite Watson's magical sleuthing ability and, if I was able to, I might have to take off at a moment's notice.

"Has it ever really worked to hurry the cats along in the past?" Tara asked.

"Not really, but I am motivated to get this wrapped up. The next week is going to be a busy one. I don't want this hanging over my head."

"Isn't the whole reason you got involved in looking in to Amy's murder after all these years because of Winifred's death?" Cassie asked.

"Yes, I suppose it is."

"And the answer to the question who killed Winifred Westminster has been answered," Cassie pointed out. "Have you stopped to consider that perhaps you are done? Maybe the cat was here to help you find Winifred's killer, not Amy's."

I made a face. "That doesn't seem right. I get what you are saying. If Winnie hadn't died, I most likely would never have started looking for Amy's killer, but now that I have, it feels wrong to just stop before we find an answer."

"It's been fifteen years," Cassie reminded me. "Maybe there isn't an answer to find. At least not anymore. Maybe whatever evidence ever existed is long gone."

"Maybe, but that doesn't mean I can't try." I glanced into the cat lounge. Watson was no longer sleeping on the sofa. I looked around the room but didn't see him. The door between the coffee bar and the cat lounge was closed, and there wasn't a door between the cat lounge and the sidewalk outside, so it wasn't as if he could have gone anywhere. I headed toward the cat lounge expecting to find him hiding behind one of the chairs, but a thorough search told me that the cat was gone.

"That makes no sense," Tara said. "There was nowhere for him to go. He has to be here somewhere."

"Do you see him?" I asked.

Tara put her hands on her hips and looked around the room. "No, but he must be somewhere." She picked up a cushion and took a peek underneath it even though it was pretty much impossible that she'd find him there.

"I think your magical kitty pulled a disappearing act," Cassie said.

"He's not that kind of magical. He can't just disappear. He has to be somewhere."

"Maybe he worked the door between the cat lounge and the bookstore open when we were talking and slipped down the hallway. Let's check the office and the storage room," Tara suggested.

A thorough search of the entire building confirmed the dread I'd begun to feel in my gut. Watson seemed to have flown the coop. My first instinct was to enlist Tansy's help in locating the little escapee, but I decided to walk around outside to see if maybe he was just lounging in the sun, which had broken through the clouds about an hour earlier. I didn't see him on the wharf or on the road that paralleled the front of the store and was about to head down the street to Herbalities, Bella and Tansy's shop, when I noticed the woman who had inquired about adopting Watson sitting on a bench in the park across from the stores on Main. It looked like she had something in her lap, so I crossed the street and headed toward her.

"You found Watson."

The woman's faded blue eyes danced with delight. "I think he found me. I was just sitting here, trying to work up the energy to complete my shopping, when he wandered up and climbed into my lap." She hugged the cat to her chest. "Are you sure he isn't available for adoption?"

I paused. I needed him to help me find Amy's killer, but I supposed once I did, he would need a home. "He isn't eligible yet, but he might be soon. Would you be willing to wait?"

"I would." The woman answered.

I looked at Watson. "Is that okay with you?"

The cat began to purr loudly.

I looked at the woman. "You have my number. Call me next week, and I should be able to provide you with an update."

I could sense the woman was not happy about me taking Watson, but after I promised again to do what I could to speed up an adoption if at all possible, she handed him over to me. I carried the cat back to Coffee Cat Books. Once we'd rounded the corner to the wharf, I loosened my grip on him, and he struggled free.

I was preparing to give chase when he walked purposely but not quickly toward the ferry office. I opened the door for him, and he slipped inside. He headed straight for a bulletin board, then swatted at a flyer for the community haunted house that had opened the night before and ran until Halloween.

"You want me to go to the haunted house?"

"Meow."

"I don't think it opens until later in the afternoon."

The cat jumped up on one of the benches provided for passengers waiting for the ferry and just looked at me. I looked more closely at the flyer. The haunted house opened at four and ran until ten. The homecoming game also started at four. I supposed I could be late to the game if Watson really did have a reason for wanting me to check out the haunted house. When it came down to it, solving Amy's murder was the most important thing.

I took the flyer down from the board and looked at it a bit more closely. Not only were the dates and times for the event listed but on the back, the volunteers were listed by name. Among the forty or so names, one stood out to me: Lexi Michaels. The haunted house didn't open to the public for a couple more hours, but I had to wonder if perhaps Lexi, as a volunteer, might already be at the community center getting things ready. Making a quick decision, I texted Tara to let her know where I was going, and then Watson and I started off in that direction.

Chapter 17

When we arrived, we found Lexi right away, chatting with a tall man in a Frankenstein costume. The green mask prevented me from identifying who he was, but there were only a handful of men over six and a half feet tall on the island, so I was sure with a little time I could figure it out. Not that knowing was important at that point, so I didn't ask any questions.

"Cait, are you here to volunteer?" Lexi asked, a gleam of hope in her eyes.

"No, I'm afraid not. I wanted to speak to you, though, if you have a minute."

Lexi looked toward a group of volunteers who were hanging a skeleton. It didn't appear they needed her help, and she must have decided so as well because she nodded and indicated I should follow her.

"So how can I help you?" she asked.

"I'm sure you know that the death of Winifred Westminster inadvertently brought Amy's murder case to the forefront after all this time."

She nodded. "Yes, but I thought Winifred Westminster was killed by someone other than whoever killed Amy. I've only heard fragments of rumors and am far from having all, or even any, of the facts, but everyone is saying the cases aren't linked."

"You are correct. The person who killed Winnie is not the same person who killed Amy."

"Do you know who did it?" Lexi asked. "There are all sorts of theories being passed around, but other than the story that the two deaths were not linked, as everyone suspected, no one seems to know who actually killed Winnie."

I supposed that Finn might not want that information making the rounds just yet, so I simply answered that I wasn't a hundred percent certain what had really happened in the case of Winnie's murder but had decided to focus on Amy's instead.

"I don't know who killed Amy," Lexi said. "If I did, I would have said so."

"I believe that you don't know who killed her, but I suspect you do know which staff member at the high school she was sleeping with."

Lexi lowered her eyes. "I don't want to get anyone in trouble."

"What if the guy she was sleeping with killed her?"

"He didn't. He wasn't even on the island when Amy died."

Okay, I supposed that was a clue. "Okay, so maybe this man didn't kill her, but maybe someone else who knew about the affair did. Maybe Coach Brown, for example."

Lexi visibly pulled away. "Coach Brown was a roach, but he didn't kill Amy."

"Are you sure? He was at the party on the night Amy died. He might have found out she was sleeping it off in the bedroom upstairs, found his way into the room, and killed her."

Lexi shook her head. "I was really upset when I found out Amy was upstairs with her conquest of the evening, so I made a really strong drink and went outside to sit on the tree swing at the back of the property. Coach Brown came out of the house and saw me sitting there. He came over and started up a conversation with me. We talked for a while, and then he left. There is no way he could have killed Amy."

"You said Amy was upstairs with a guy. What guy?"

Lexi shrugged. "Just some guy. I don't remember who."

"How did you know she was upstairs with anyone?"

She shrugged again. "I don't know. I guess someone must have told me so. Or maybe I saw them go up to the room. It was a long time ago, and I had been drinking. Do you remember every single detail of every single thing you said, saw, and did fifteen years ago?"

"Well, no, but given the fact that Amy was found dead the next morning, I would think the identity of the person Amy went upstairs with would be significant enough that you would remember."

"Okay, so maybe I saw something. On the night of the party, I was hoping to hook up with this guy I had been crushing on in a major way. Up until that point, I hadn't told anyone about my feelings for this guy, not even Amy, but we'd run into each other at the homecoming game, and he'd mentioned that he was planning to show up at Lance's party and maybe he'd see me there. I took that to indicate that he felt about me the way I felt about him, but when he showed up, he seemed to have eyes for someone else. I realized that the reason this guy had shown up at the party wasn't because of me, but because of this other girl, so I poured myself that strong drink and went outside. While I was out there, I saw Amy come out onto the deck and lean over. She said something to someone who must have been standing in the yard below her. I watched as a guy in dark clothes climbed the ladder and disappeared into the room with Amy."

"Are you sure you have no idea who Amy invited up to the room?"

"I said I didn't."

"Could it have been Brock Stevenson? He was dating Amy right up until the time of the party, but they'd recently broken up. She came with Gavin Prescott and Brock came with Jamie Fisher, but I remember him glaring at Amy while she tried to pick up Chase. I considered the fact that he might have killed Amy in a jealous rage."

Lexi smiled slightly and shook her head. "Brock would never kill Amy. He loved her, and I think she loved him too. If she hadn't died, I think they would have eventually gotten back together. Amy was seriously out of control when she died. I don't know exactly what was going on, but she seemed to be pushing away those of us who loved her the most in order to spend time with people who just wanted to use her."

"What about Chase?"

"What about him?"

"Do you think he might have been the one to climb the ladder and join Amy? She had been all over him for most of the evening."

Lexi shrugged. "I don't know. Maybe."

"If you had to guess, who do you think you saw?"

Lexi crossed her arms over her chest. "I don't know. Stop asking me that. I just saw some guy. It might even have been a girl. Maybe you should talk to Liza. She was angry with Amy all evening, and it would be just like her to hold a pillow over someone's face." Lexi took a step away. "I need to go. The others are waiting for me."

I had other questions I would have liked to have asked, but Lexi walked away, so short of tackling her to the ground, this conversation was over. I decided to go look for Watson, who I found curled up in a bin full of dismembered body parts. I retrieved my sidekick kitty, and we headed back to the bookstore.

"So, were you able to track down Lexi?" Tara asked when I joined her at the coffee counter.

"I did." I explained everything we'd talked about. "Tripp identified five suspects during the original investigation, and it seems that any of them could have been the one to climb the ladder and join Amy in the bedroom."

"Do you know if Finn ever talked to Chase?" Tara asked. "I know he is hanging around offshore on his yacht, but it seems that Finn could take the sheriff's boat out to the yacht and chat with him if he felt it was important."

"I'm not sure," I answered. "I suppose I should check in with Finn anyway, so we can figure out where we stand at this point." I huffed out a breath.

"But let's do that later. I don't think this case is solvable in one day, no matter how much I hoped it was unless we stumble upon a significant lead, so let's go ahead and close up. I don't want to be late for the game."

Chapter 18

By the time game time rolled around, the last of the clouds had cleared, and it turned out to be a beautiful day. Cassie had gone off to sit with some of her own friends, but Siobhan, Danny, Tara, Cody, and I all sat together. Finn was going to be late, so Siobhan was saving him a seat.

"Aiden didn't want to come to the game?" I asked Danny.

"He's staying back at the bar to make sure everything is ready for the party," Danny said. "You know he never was in to football."

"That's true, but I would think he'd prefer to get out and spend time with his family rather than staying in the bar by himself."

"There were a few people with him when I left. Do you remember Duncan Jones? He was in Aiden's class."

"Vaguely," I answered.

"He married Connie Pane from my class. She wanted to come to the game, but Duncan wasn't in to it, so the last time I saw him, Duncan was sitting at the bar chatting with Aiden."

"Didn't you used to date Connie Pane?" Tara asked.

"For a while. In fact, now that I think about it, I'm pretty sure we hooked up for the first time the night of the homecoming party."

I had no idea when Connie and Danny had first hooked up, but now that Danny mentioned it, I did remember seeing Connie at the party. Like the other dozens and dozens of partygoers who had not made it to our suspect list because they hadn't seemed to have had a motive to kill Amy and they hadn't been on the island when Winnie died, Connie had been at the party and could very well have seen something.

"Connie was friends with Liza Tisdale." I looked at Danny. "You used to date Liza too."

Danny shrugged. "I got around."

"Are you going somewhere with this?" Siobhan asked.

I slowly tipped my head to the left. "I'm not sure. Bringing up Connie's name seems to have ignited a memory, but I'm still trying to work out what it is I remember." I looked at Danny. "Did you bring a date to the party that night?"

"Brittany Everson. Though shortly after we arrived, she took off with a bunch of her girlfriends, which is why I started talking to Connie. I'd become friends with her while dating Liza and we got along okay. Connie seemed to be on her own for some reason, so we ended up hanging out. I think we dated for a month or two. It was never anything serious."

The team filed onto the field at that moment, and everyone got to their feet to cheer them on. At halftime, we were behind by two points. Both teams seemed to have brought their A game. It would be interesting to see how the second half went.

"I'm going to go grab some nachos from the snack bar. Does anyone else want anything?" I asked.

No one did, although Cody offered to go with me if I wanted. I told him I was fine on my own and just asked him to be sure to save my seat. The line was longer than I'd anticipated, but I decided to wait anyway, so I got into line behind a group from the rival team and tried to ignore their trash talk. When Owen got into line behind me, I turned and smiled at him.

"How are you handling things?" I asked.

"Okay. Actually, I'm not okay. In fact, I am very much not okay, but I'll survive." He pulled an envelope out of his pocket. "I know you wanted to see any photos I had from the party, so I looked through my archives. I don't have many, but I figured you'd be here today, so I brought what I had."

I took the envelope from Owen's hand. "Thank you. I appreciate that. I'll look them over and get them back to you."

"Don't bother. I find that the evening depicted in these photos is not one I want to remember."

After I bought my nachos and returned to my seat, I asked Cody to hold my hot, cheesy snack and opened the envelope. It was odd to be transported back in time to that pivotal evening. Everyone looked so young, and what was up with Cody's hair? I had to chuckle.

"Not the best photo of me," Cody admitted.

"No, it isn't," I agreed.

I continued to sort through the photos, which mainly consisted of random shots of guests doing silly things or making funny faces. I was pretty sure the answer to the question who killed Amy Anderson would not be found in the photos, but then I noticed something interesting. Archie was standing in the background of a photo of Brock chugging a beer. He was staring at Amy with a look of intensity on his face that wouldn't be expected from a party situation. Across the room stood Lexi, who seemed to be watching Archie. I flipped through the photos to find other examples of Archie watching Amy, while Lexi watched Archie. I remembered that Lexi had said that she had hoped to make a connection of the romantic sort with a guy she had been friends with but from whom she wanted more. I also remembered that Owen had mentioned that Lexi and Archie were friends. Could Archie have been the guy Lexi was lusting after? And if so, had Archie, in turn, been lusting after Amy? Seemed unlikely but not impossible.

I wasn't sure how or even if this interesting revelation played into Amy's death in any way, but suddenly I felt the need to have another conversation with Lexi. Finn had just arrived, so I pulled him aside and shared my thoughts. He agreed that there could have been something going on between Archie, Lexi, and Amy. I told him I wanted to head over to the haunted house to try to talk to Lexi again and he offered to come with me, but I was afraid that if Lexi did know something or was guilty of anything, she wouldn't talk if Finn was there. He agreed to my plan to accompany me wearing a disguise. Cody and

Siobhan wanted to come along as well but would wait in the car.

At the haunted house, I looked around for Lexi. It took me a while to find her because everyone had put on costumes, but eventually, I was able to spot her. "Can I talk to you for a minute?" I asked.

She looked around. "I'm sort of busy."

"It will only take a minute."

She blew out a breath. "Okay. But a minute is really all I have." I led her away from the crowd. "So how can I help you now? I assume this is about Amy's murder again?"

"It is." A man dressed in a monster outfit, who I knew was Finn scooted closer. Lexi didn't seem to notice him; there were people in costume everywhere. "I remembered you said that you saw someone climb the ladder and join Amy in the bedroom after you went outside to have a drink."

"Yes. That's right."

"And you said that you didn't know who it was."

She nodded. "That's right."

"Could it have been Archie Baldwin?"

Lexi paled. I could see in her eyes that it was true.

"I don't know who it was," she denied. "It was dark and I had been drinking."

"I wondered if you remembered how Amy died," I continued, ignoring the fact that Lexi obviously wanted to flee.

"She was strangled. Everyone knows that. It was all over the newspapers, so you didn't need to pull me away from my job to ask me that."

"I know. It's just that when we spoke earlier, you made a comment about Liza Tisdale being mad enough to smother Amy with a pillow."

Lexi snorted out a shallow laugh. "Oh, that." She waved her hand dismissively. "I guess it was just a slip of the tongue. Like I said, everyone knows Amy was strangled. Now, if that is all…"

"I know you had feelings for Archie."

Lexi gasped. She looked like she was going to cry. "So?" she asked in a small voice.

"When you saw Archie climb the ladder and join Amy in the bedroom, you were upset. More than upset. You were drunk and angry and probably feeling betrayed. You probably waited for Archie to climb back down the ladder and leave. When he did, you went up the ladder to confront Amy. I imagine you found her sleeping and, without even stopping to think about what you were doing, you held a pillow over her face and smothered her to death."

A tear slid down Lexi's face, followed by another. I waited for her to speak. If nothing else, I figured she'd deny my allegations. "Amy knew how I felt about Archie. I'd told her everything. I even told her that I hoped that he would be the one I would finally lose my virginity to. She didn't care about him. She just wanted to hurt me. I knew that the minute I saw them together." She began to sob. "I didn't mean to kill Amy. I was just so mad and so very, very drunk. I didn't even realize what I was doing until it was too late. After I saw Amy was dead, I went back down the ladder and went home. I thought about telling someone what I'd done, but I was scared. I was just a kid. A kid who lost her mind and did a terrible thing."

I looked at Finn, who had been listening in. "Is that enough?"

He took off his monster mask and stepped forward. "Lexi Michaels, you are under arrest for the murder of Amy Anderson. You have the right to remain silent…"

I watched as Finn led Lexi to his cruiser. Siobhan and Cody were waiting in Cody's car, so I headed in that direction. I wished I could say that I was happy to have solved the mystery of Amy Anderson's murder, but the truth of the matter was, all I felt was sad and sort of empty inside.

Chapter 19

Monday, October 28

It did my heart good to see the bar so packed with friends and family who had turned out for Cassie's twenty-first birthday party. It had been sort of a last-minute deal, and I wasn't sure how many of Cassie's friends would be able to make it, but apparently, my baby sister was quite the popular young woman. The only family member who had not made it yet was Finn, who had called to say that he had a conference call he couldn't miss but would meet us at O'Malley's. Maggie and Michael were staying at the house she'd given Siobhan and Finn, so my older sister and her baby had come to the bar with them.

"Thank you so much." Cassie hugged me. "I didn't think I wanted a party, but now that everyone is here, I am having the best time."

"I'm so glad. I can't believe my baby sister is twenty-one."

"I haven't been your baby sister for a long time," Cassie reminded me.

"Sorry, kiddo, but you are the youngest, which will forever make you the baby."

Cassie groaned.

"I noticed Mom come in earlier but didn't see Gabe," I said, referring to the man who was now her new husband.

"He will be by later. His daughter is visiting, and he is having dinner with her." Cassie waved at three women about her age who had just walked in. "I should go say hi." She hugged me again. "Thank you for everything."

I headed to the bar, where Tara was chatting with Danny. I'd been trying to figure out if there was anything other than friendship going on between the two of them, but I just couldn't be sure. Tara seemed to be intentionally evasive about the time the two of them had been spending together, and Danny simply shrugged when I'd commented that the two of them were spending more time together than they had in the past, but from what I had observed, they were very close to becoming an item once again. I wished I knew whether to be happy or scared about that.

I slid onto the barstool next to Tara, who was smiling from cheek to cheek. "It looks like everything came together very nicely," she said.

"It's great, and Cassie is very happy."

"How did your meeting with the woman who wants to adopt Watson go?" Tara asked.

"It went well. She adores Watson, and he adores her. I'm not sure if I mentioned the fact that she's elderly and wanted a mellow cat. Watson fits that bill perfectly."

"Do you think the cats who come in and out of your life only possess these unique abilities while they are with you? I mean, do you think they understand their new owners after they leave you?"

"I don't know. I know that Ebenezer is as sharp as he ever was," I said, referring to my friend Balthazar Pottage's cat. "Of course, he was a unique cat from the first moment I met him. I guess it would be interesting to look up some of my old sleuthing partners to see if they continued to sleuth once they moved on to new homes."

"It looks like Cody is waving to you."

I turned around and waved to let him know I was on my way. Then I looked at Danny. "When you get caught up, I'll take a white wine," I said to the younger of my two brothers. "I'm going to go to see what Cody wants, but I'll be back after that."

The room was crowded enough by this point that I had to maneuver my way through the masses on my way to where Cody was standing near the door leading out to the parking lot. He was speaking to a tall man with dark hair who I didn't recognize.

"Cait." Cody held out his hand to me. "This is my friend, Andy. We went to high school together."

"I'm happy to meet you." I smiled and shook his hand.

"I went out to the car to grab the extra paper plates we brought when I noticed Andy walking down the street and invited him in."

"So this is Danny Hart's little sister? I've heard a lot about you."

"You have?"

"Cody mentioned you on occasion back when the two of us were on the cross-country team together."

I glanced at Cody and smiled. "You don't say. To be honest, I wasn't sure I was even on Cody's radar back then."

"Oh, you were," the man assured me.

I bumped a hip into Cody's playfully. "Good to know."

"Andy and I were talking about going over to San Juan Island to play some golf tomorrow if you don't have other plans for me," Cody said.

"That sounds like fun, and no, I don't have other plans. Have a wonderful time." I glanced across the room. Finn had just arrived. "I need to ask Finn a question." I turned to Andy. "It was nice meeting you." I kissed Cody on the cheek and went across the room.

"Any luck?" I asked Finn, who was just greeting Siobhan and Connor.

"Actually, yes." He looked around the room. "Let's head back to the office so we can talk without being overheard."

I nodded and followed Finn down the hallway. I knew that Finn had been speaking to the feds about Archie. "So?" I asked when we were alone.

"According to the sheriff, Archie is in federal custody."

I blew out a breath. "That's great. Do you think he will do time in prison?"

"I don't know. The sheriff didn't know, but he didn't think so. Archie is a valuable NSA asset whose expertise is not easily replaceable. If he had even a moderately fair reason for killing Ms. Westminster, I doubt he'll do time behind bars."

"That doesn't seem right."

Finn nodded. "I don't disagree, but sometimes things don't work out in a way that is fair or right. I suppose at this point, Archie's fate is in the hands of others. I think we should just call it a day and move on."

I frowned. "I guess. Is Lexi still in custody on San Juan Island?"

Finn nodded. "She is. She confessed to everything and is working out a deal for a reduced sentence. She was a minor when she killed Amy, so that will help." Finn looked around the room. "Good turnout. It looks like you and Siobhan managed to get hold of everyone you intended." Suddenly, Finn, the deputy had been replaced by Finn, the brother-in-law.

"We do have a good turnout," I agreed. "And Danny and Tara did such a good job with the decorations. Oh, and the cake Maggie made is fabulous."

"Everything is perfect," Finn agreed. "Which is why I am going to suggest that you go out there and enjoy yourself and try not to think about murder and mayhem."

I supposed that Finn had a point. I'd done my job, and now it was time to enjoy my family and friends.

Chapter 20

Later that evening, after Cody and I got home from the party, we bundled up to take Max out for a short run. Despite all the rain we'd been having lately, the sky was brilliant with stars this evening. It had been a hectic yet fun evening. Between the party for homecoming and the birthday party tonight, I was on the verge of being partied out, and we still had Halloween to get through.

"I never did ask you about your visit with your mother," I said to Cody. "You arrived back on the island in the middle of Winnie's murder investigation, and I guess I was distracted."

"It went fine. You know I miss you when I am away, but I feel that I owe my mother a visit or two each year."

"I get that. If I had a kid who moved clear across the country, I'd hope they'd visit me as well. And your mom can always come and visit us here if she wants. We won't have room for guests until after the remodel in Mr. Parsons's house is done, but after that, we should have plenty of room."

"She mentioned coming for a visit at some point. Maybe over the summer. In the meantime, she really wants us to go to Florida for Thanksgiving. She actually wanted us for Christmas, but I told her that we had already made plans on the island for then."

I frowned. "Does it seem to you that your mother is a lot more interested in having you come for a visit since we became a couple than she was before we got engaged?"

"She wants to be sure we have a schedule of sorts set up for the holidays before the grandchildren are born. I think she thinks that if we don't have a system in place, she'll never get to see her grandbabies."

"Did you tell her that we have no immediate plans to have children?"

Cody nodded. "I did. But you know how those things go."

Those things? I certainly hoped that Cody's mother had not put the idea of starting a family in Cody's mind. I loved him, and someday I wanted us to have a family, but that someday was definitely not this day. Or any day in close proximity to this day, for that matter. Still, I supposed that having holidays in Florida was only fair. I was just glad we were talking Thanksgiving and not Christmas. Although if we went for Thanksgiving, that might very well mean we'd end up spending our first anniversary there. I supposed we could work around that to avoid the situation.

"So what do you think?" Cody asked when I didn't respond immediately.

"I guess having Thanksgiving with your mom is fair, but that doesn't give us a lot of time to plan a trip. And November 21st is our first wedding anniversary. I'd like it to be just the two of us for that."

Cody tightened his hand on mine. "I thought about that. I was thinking we could go to the Bahamas for our anniversary, and then we could arrive at my mom's on the twenty-seventh. We could stay a couple of days and be back on Madrona Island by the following Monday."

"Seems doable." I glanced at Cody. "From your tone of voice, however, somehow I'm sensing a catch."

"My cousin, Maddie, had a baby a few months ago."

"That's nice," I said. I tried to remember if I'd met Maddie, but I was pretty sure I hadn't.

"She's in the Air Force."

"I see." I stopped walking and turned to look at Cody. "Is there a reason you are telling me this?"

"Maddie has been deployed. She leaves the day after Thanksgiving."

"That sounds like it will be rough with a new baby."

"It will be, but she knew it was coming. I think she is prepared to do whatever's necessary to honor her commitments."

"Okay," I hedged. "I guess that is good."

"It is. It's just that Maddie's husband, Matt, is also in the Air Force. He's currently overseas."

I just stared at Cody, waiting for the other shoe to drop. "And?"

"And while he is coming home from overseas duty soon, he won't be home until just after the new year. That creates a problem because Maddie will need to find someone to watch Sammy until Matt gets home."

"And?" I asked as tension coiled in my belly.

"And she wondered if we could babysit for the six weeks until Matt gets home."

I simply stood there on the beach with my mouth hanging open.

"It will just be for six weeks," Cody continued. "Sammy is so cute. You are going to love him. And it will be good practice for us, for when we have our own kids."

"You already told her we would do it." I realized this was true even before I said it.

Cody hung his head. "I did. I shouldn't have told Maddie I would do it without talking to you first, but she seemed so desperate. She begged me to please do her this one small favor, and I found myself agreeing."

"You agreed that we would babysit an infant for six weeks without asking me first?"

Cody cringed. "I did."

I didn't respond.

"The timing works out perfectly because we can bring Sammy back with us after our trip to Florida for Thanksgiving."

I still didn't say anything.

Cody put his arms around me. "I'm sorry. I messed up, and I know it. I can call Maddie and tell her we can't keep Sammy. I'm sure she will understand."

No, I knew deep in my heart she wouldn't. "Who is going to watch Sammy when we are both at work?"

"I'll find a babysitter. Maybe the woman Siobhan uses for Connor."

This husband of mine was going to owe me so big. "Okay."

"Okay?" Cody placed a finger under his chin and tipped up my face toward his. He looked me directly in the eye.

I nodded slightly. "Okay."

UP NEXT FROM KATHI DALEY BOOKS

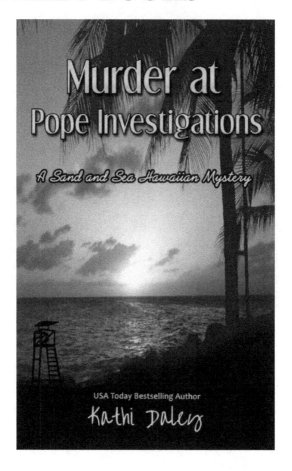

Preview:

Tuesday, June 25

I should have been surprised to find the tall man with the dark skin and dark hair dead just inside the front door when I arrived at Pope Investigations, the detective agency where I work with my father, Keanu Pope, but he wasn't the first gunshot victim I'd stumbled upon this month. He was, in fact, the third. The remains of the first gunshot victim had been found on the beach behind the oceanfront condo where I live with my cousin, Kekoa. My brother, Jason, a detective for the Honolulu Police Department, figured the murder was a random act that I'd just happened to have stumbled upon. When the second body was found propped up on the lifeguard tower at The Dolphin Bay Resort, where I'd been working just one day a week since taking the full-time position at the detective agency, my brother considered that I might be connected to both men in some way. Jason learned that the first victim was a retired Air Force Master Sergeant who was vacationing on Oahu, and the second was a nightclub owner living in Honolulu. As hard as he tried, he couldn't find a connection between the two men, or between the two men and me. After several days, he'd moved onto other theories. But now that a third victim had been found at the location where I spent the majority of my time, in my mind there was no denying that someone was leaving me bodies.

After checking for a pulse to confirm that the man was actually dead, I called Jason, who promised to be right over. I was about to walk around to the beach in order to get away from the gruesome sight when a dark four-door sedan pulled into the drive. I realized this was my first client of the morning, so I took a deep breath and headed toward the car, intent on heading the woman off before she noticed the murder victim just inside the front door.

"Hokulani Palakiko?" I asked, greeting the dark-haired woman dressed in a colorful dress in a Hawaiian print.

"Yes." The woman leaned out through her open driver's door window. "You can call me Hoku."

"My name is Lani. Lani Pope. I'm afraid we have a bit of a situation this morning, and I'm going to need to reschedule."

"Situation?" The woman looked toward the front of the building for the first time.

"We've had a break-in," I decided not to mention the dead body. "I'm so sorry for the inconvenience, but if you leave a number where you can be reached, I'll call you with a new time to meet."

The woman furrowed her brow. "You do understand that my husband is missing?"

I nodded. "Yes. My father filled me in."

"I understand that a break-in is inconvenient, but I would think that a missing person would be a bit more of a priority."

"Yes, I see your point. It is just that the HPD officer I spoke to told me to wait for him and not to touch anything. Perhaps we can meet later today. I'm not sure if it will work to meet here at the office, but I would be willing to meet you at your home." I glanced at my watch. It was just ten o'clock now. "I should be done here by noon."

The woman frowned. She huffed out a breath, drummed her fingers on the steering wheel in front of her, and, it seemed, generally did everything she could to convey her annoyance. "Okay." She adjusted her sunglasses and turned to look directly at me. "I guess two hours won't make all that much difference, but I expect you to be prompt."

"I'll do my best."

The woman gave me her address, which luckily wasn't far from the office. I hoped she'd be long gone before Jason arrived, so I entered her phone number and home address in my phone and promised to text her with a confirmation that I would be free by twelve once I spoke to the police. She hemmed and hawed a bit more, I was sure in an effort to make certain that I understood exactly how unhappy she was with the situation, but eventually, she pulled out of the drive and headed down the highway. Minutes after she pulled away, Jason pulled into the lot in front of Pope Investigations.

I ran over to the car to greet my second oldest of five brothers. "Thank you for coming so quickly."

Jason looked toward the house. "Is Dad here?"

"He is on the South Shore this morning. I left him a message, but haven't heard back. I'm not exactly sure who he is meeting, but he mentioned something about a new client."

"And the victim?"

"Tall, male. Young looking, maybe mid-twenties. I'm pretty sure I don't know the man, but he does look a little familiar. I've tried to remember where I might have seen him, but I came up empty."

Jason turned as another HPD cruiser showed up. "Okay. I think it is best that you wait out here. Colin and I will have a look."

"I have to leave for another appointment at eleven-thirty. I can come back after I'm done if need be. I'm sure Dad will head over here once he gets my message."

Jason nodded. "Okay. I'll come back out here and talk to you once I have a chance to assess the situation. Maybe you can just wait on the lanai.

"Okay. I'll be there. If you need me, holler."

After Jason went inside, I sat down on a patio chair and checked my messages. There was a message from my dentist reminding me that it was time for a checkup and cleaning; a text from my boss at the Dolphin Bay Resort where I still worked on Saturdays as a water safety officer, letting me know he had made up the schedule for the Fourth of July and that I was going to be needed for a ten hour shift; and a missed call from Dad. I opened my phone app and called him back. He picked up on the first ring.

"Hi, Dad. Did you get my message?"

"I did. Are you okay?"

"I'm fine. Jason and Colin are here. I'm waiting outside."

Dad blew out a breath loud enough for me to hear, although, without corresponding facial cues, I was unable to tell if it was a breath of relief, anxiety, or irritation.

"Three murder victims in three weeks all placed so as to make it likely that they'd be found by you is not a coincidence. I'm not liking this one bit. I think we should talk to Jason about protective custody for you."

"No, thanks," I responded immediately. "I can take care of myself. Plus, I realized after I found the body this morning that the murders have been spaced ten days apart. Exactly ten days apart. That means that we have ten days to figure out who is doing this before someone else is killed."

"I guess you have a point, if the killer follows his pattern, there won't be another murder for ten days. Still, I want to know that you are safe at all times."

"You can't know that I am safe at all times any more than I can know that you are safe at all times, but I will be extra careful. I promise."

"Is Kekoa there with you?"

Kekoa worked full-time for the Dolphin Bay Resort and part-time for us answering phones and taking care of the filing and bookkeeping.

"No. She planned to be in this afternoon. I'll call her and let her know not to bother to come in today."

"I just finished up here and am on my way back. I should be there in an hour."

"Just so you know," I added, "the new client with the missing husband you told me about showed up after I arrived but before Jason pulled in. I met her at her car and told her we'd had a break-in. I didn't mention the murder. She agreed to meet with me at her home later today since the office was unavailable. I am meeting her at noon."

"I guess that will be okay. Generally speaking, I am not a fan of you meeting clients at their homes unless I am along, but Hokulani Palakiko seems harmless enough, and I know she is concerned about her husband. I should be back by the time you return from the interview so we can discuss a strategy later this afternoon."

"Okay."

"And Lani. Be careful. I know that you are a capable young woman, but it seems as if you have somehow garnered the attention of a very dangerous person who has already killed three people and most likely won't hesitate to kill again."

"I know. I'll be careful." After I hung up with Dad, I got up from the patio chair and walked out onto the beach. I let the warm water roll over my bare feet and then called Kekoa to fill her in. I explained about the break-in and the body inside the entry and suggested she hold off coming in to take care of the bookkeeping until tomorrow. Like everyone else, she was concerned that this serial killer seemed to be focused in on me, but I assured her I would be fine and we would talk later.

Jason walked out the back door and onto the beach just as I was finishing my conversation with Kekoa. "So?" I asked.

"The victim was shot at close range. It appears a small caliber handgun was used. We'll know more when we get the ballistics report back. It appears, based on lack of blood splatter, that the man was shot elsewhere and then dumped the same as the other two. With this third victim, I am more convinced than ever that you are somehow at the center of whatever is going on. We might want to consider protective custody. Did you get ahold of Dad?"

I nodded. "He is on his way from the South Shore, and there is no way I am going to sit around in a safe house when there is some wacko running around killing people and then leaving the remains for me like some sort of a sick gift. I need to meet with our new client, but I will come back when I'm done, and we can talk about this some more. I'm not sure what I can tell you that would help you to figure out who is doing this, but I am certain that we need to find the guy before he kills again."

"I agree. And we'll talk some more about protective custody when I am done here as well."

I was never going to agree to protective custody. I knew it, and he knew it, so I didn't bother to argue. I simply said my goodbyes and headed toward my car. Having a missing person to look for seemed like a distraction at this point, but Hoku was our client, and she was paying us good money to find her husband, who I was fairly sure she was more than just a little worried about.

I followed the directions provided by the Maps app on my phone to a large two-story house located in a nice neighborhood just a few blocks from the sea. Hoku's car was in the drive, so I pulled up on the street. One of these days, I was going to trade in my old Jeep for something that wasn't older than I was, but I never seemed to have enough income to deal with car payments, so a new car would need to wait.

I walked up the shrub-lined walkway toward the covered porch. I rang the bell and then waited.

"Oh good, you came," the woman said, stepping aside. "Is your father with you?"

"He couldn't make it, but he does plan to consult with me about a strategy once I get the basic information we will need to begin our search."

The woman frowned. "I see. How old are you?"

"Old enough," I assured the woman. Being a small woman, barely five feet in height, often led people to believe I was younger than I actually am. I pulled out a notepad and pen. "Is there somewhere you would like to sit while we chat?"

"How about out on the lanai? It is a beautiful day today. Not at all as hot as it has been."

I had to agree with that. It was a beautiful day. "So I have your husband's name, age, and occupation, but I'd like to go over everything again to make sure there are no errors."

"Okay."

I read my notes which told me that Kinsley Palakiko was a sixty-eight-year-old retired airline pilot who was last seen on Saturday around lunchtime when he left his home to do errands. He never came home, nor did he make the tee time he had set up with a friend on Sunday morning. Hoku called and spoke to my father yesterday when her husband still had not called or shown up. He'd completed a basic questionnaire over the phone. He'd traced the man's phone, tracked his credit cards, and conducted a GPS search for his car. It was determined that the phone had been turned off, the GPS on the car was disabled, and the credit cards had not been used. We did live on an island, and the man was a retired airline pilot, so Dad checked with the airlines that served the island, but none reported activity from Kinsley in over a month. Hoku verified that the two of them had gone to the mainland for a week just about a month ago and that neither of them had traveled from the island since. She also verified that Kinsley had access to a private plane owned by a close friend, so dad had called the friend and verified that Kinsley hadn't borrowed the plane recently.

"If your husband felt the need to get away and didn't want to be found for whatever reason, where would he go?" I asked.

"You think my husband is off having some sort of a fling?"

"Not necessarily," I answered. "However, statistically speaking, more missing persons turn out not to have been the victim of foul play than turn out to have been. It is smart to look at all options."

"So you think Kinsley is just fine. You think he has put me through what is by far the worst few days of my life for nothing."

"Again, I'm not necessarily saying that." I paused and looked at the woman who seemed to be more angry than scared. "When your husband didn't come home after two days, why did you call Pope Investigations? Why didn't you call the police?"

The woman lowered her gaze but didn't respond right away.

"You don't think he has met with foul play either. You think he simply took off and you want him found. You may even believe that he is missing because he is engaged in some sort of illegal activity and you didn't want to get the authorities involved."

"That's a lot of speculation," the woman accused.

"Perhaps. But I'm not wrong, am I?"

"Kinsley likes to gamble. He isn't very good at it and has lost most of our retirement savings over the past couple of years. He'd been out late on Friday, and we didn't speak, but when he came to bed, I could smell the smoke and alcohol that accompany a back room poker game, so I knew. He left around lunchtime on Saturday, simply saying that he had errands he needed to do. He didn't elaborate or say when he'd be home, but I assumed he'd be home in a few hours. When he didn't come home at all that day, I assumed his errands had led to a Saturday night poker game. I tried calling him about a million times, but the calls went straight to voicemail. I also checked our credit card charges, and when I realized there were none, I checked our checking account. Kinsley took out two thousand dollars on the day before he disappeared. I waited until Monday, hoping he would show up, but when he didn't, I decided to call your father. Kinsley has gone off on gambling binges in the past, but this time feels different. For one thing, he has been away longer than usual. For another, it seems very odd to me that he would leave his friend waiting for him at the golf course. You would think, at the very least, he would have called to cancel that."

I made a few notes and then looked up at the woman. "So if your husband is just off gambling somewhere, which it sounds like he very well may be, why did you think we would be able to find him when you couldn't?"

"Finding people is your job. I figured you'd have a few tricks that I didn't know to try."

I supposed we did have a few tricks that the missing man's wife didn't know to try, but now that I suspected he had taken off on his own free will, I wasn't sure I wanted to get in the middle of a marital spat. Still, there was a slim possibility that the man really had met with foul play. And Hoku did make a good point that it was odd that he had stood up his friend who was waiting at the golf course. If he planned to sneak away for a gambling spree, it seemed to me that he would, at the very least, have texted his friend to cancel the game rather than leaving him high and dry. I asked the woman several more questions, mostly relating to her husband's friends, lodging preferences, and financial situation. I promised to do what I could and to call her with an update by the following morning. I also took down the information relating to his car. It wouldn't hurt to ask my brothers and friends with HPD to keep an eye out for it. As I drove back to Pope Investigations, I made a mental list of people to talk to. If the man was a gambler, I was sure my friend, Emmy Jean Thornton, would know the guy. On the surface, Emmy Jean was a sassy southern sex kitten, but beneath the Dolly Parton exterior, was a shrewd woman who could out drink and out gamble most of the men on the island.

Books by Kathi Daley
Come for the murder, stay for the romance

Zoe Donovan Cozy Mystery:
Halloween Hijinks
The Trouble With Turkeys
Christmas Crazy
Cupid's Curse
Big Bunny Bump-off
Beach Blanket Barbie
Maui Madness
Derby Divas
Haunted Hamlet
Turkeys, Tuxes, and Tabbies
Christmas Cozy
Alaskan Alliance
Matrimony Meltdown
Soul Surrender
Heavenly Honeymoon
Hopscotch Homicide
Ghostly Graveyard
Santa Sleuth
Shamrock Shenanigans
Kitten Kaboodle
Costume Catastrophe
Candy Cane Caper
Holiday Hangover
Easter Escapade
Camp Carter
Trick or Treason
Reindeer Roundup
Hippity Hoppity Homicide

Firework Fiasco
Henderson House
Holiday Hostage
Lunacy Lake
Celtic Christmas – *December 2019*

Zimmerman Academy The New Normal
Zimmerman Academy New Beginnings
Ashton Falls Cozy Cookbook

Tj Jensen Paradise Lake Mystery:

Pumpkins in Paradise
Snowmen in Paradise
Bikinis in Paradise
Christmas in Paradise
Puppies in Paradise
Halloween in Paradise
Treasure in Paradise
Fireworks in Paradise
Beaches in Paradise
Thanksgiving in Paradise – *Fall 2019*

Whales and Tails Cozy Mystery:

Romeow and Juliet
The Mad Catter
Grimm's Furry Tail
Much Ado About Felines
Legend of Tabby Hollow
Cat of Christmas Past
A Tale of Two Tabbies
The Great Catsby
Count Catula
The Cat of Christmas Present

A Winter's Tail
The Taming of the Tabby
Frankencat
The Cat of Christmas Future
Farewell to Felines
A Whisker in Time
The Catsgiving Feast
A Whale of a Tail
The Catnap Before Christmas – *December 2019*

Writers' Retreat Mystery:
First Case
Second Look
Third Strike
Fourth Victim
Fifth Night
Sixth Cabin
Seventh Chapter
Eighth Witness
Ninth Grave

Rescue Alaska Mystery:
Finding Justice
Finding Answers
Finding Courage
Finding Christmas
Finding Shelter – *Fall 2019*

A Tess and Tilly Mystery:
The Christmas Letter
The Valentine Mystery
The Mother's Day Mishap
The Halloween House

The Thanksgiving Trip
The Saint Paddy's Promise
The Halloween Haunting – *Fall 2019*

The Inn at Holiday Bay:
Boxes in the Basement
Letters in the Library
Message in the Mantel
Answers in the Attic
Haunting in the Hallway – *August 2019*
Pilgrim in the Parlor – *October 2019*
Note in the Nutcracker – *December 2019*

The Hathaway Sisters:
Harper
Harlow

Haunting by the Sea:
Homecoming by the Sea
Secrets by the Sea
Missing by the Sea
Betrayal by the Sea
Christmas by the Sea – *Fall 2019*

Sand and Sea Hawaiian Mystery:
Murder at Dolphin Bay
Murder at Sunrise Beach
Murder at the Witching Hour
Murder at Christmas

Murder at Turtle Cove
Murder at Water's Edge
Murder at Midnight
Murder at Pope Investigations – *July 2019*

Seacliff High Mystery:
The Secret
The Curse
The Relic
The Conspiracy
The Grudge
The Shadow
The Haunting

Road to Christmas Romance:
Road to Christmas Past

USA Today best-selling author Kathi Daley lives in beautiful Lake Tahoe with her husband Ken. When she isn't writing, she likes spending time hiking the miles of desolate trails surrounding her home. She has authored more than a hundred books in eleven series, including Zoe Donovan Cozy Mysteries, Whales and Tails Island Mysteries, Tess and Tilly Cozy Mysteries, Sand and Sea Hawaiian Mysteries, Tj Jensen Paradise Lake Series, Inn at Holiday Bay Cozy Mysteries, Writers' Retreat Southern Seashore Mysteries, Rescue Alaska Paranormal Mysteries, Haunting by the Sea Paranormal Mysteries, Family Ties Mystery Romances, and Seacliff High Teen Mysteries. Find out more about her books at www.kathidaley.com

Stay up-to-date:
Newsletter, *The Daley Weekly*
http://eepurl.com/NRPDf
Webpage – www.kathidaley.com
Facebook at Kathi Daley Books –
www.facebook.com/kathidaleybooks
Kathi Daley Books Group Page –
https://www.facebook.com/groups/569578823146850/
E-mail – kathidaley@kathidaley.com
Twitter at Kathi Daley@kathidaley –
https://twitter.com/kathidaley
Amazon Author Page –
https://www.amazon.com/author/kathidaley
BookBub –
https://www.bookbub.com/authors/kathi-daley

202